I0680966

DESIGNER BABIES
Volume Two
Growing Pains

David Witt

Fat Chance Publishing

This is a work of fiction. Names, characters, places, and incidents either are the product of the author's imagination or are used fictitiously. Any resemblance to actual persons, living or dead, events, or locales is entirely coincidental.

DESIGNER BABIES VOLUME TWO GROWING PAINS

Copyright © 2021 by David Witt.

ISBN 978-1-7342023-4-2

FIRST EDITION

Cover Design by Matt Witt

Attributions:

"Vecteezy.com"

"Designed by vectorstock (Image #25179632 at Vector-Stock.com)"

To Karen, my awesome and lovely wife without who's unending support this novel would not have been possible. From reading rough drafts to suggesting ways to publicize my work, she was an important part of bringing this book to market. She has been a constant source of encouragement throughout our life journey together, and I can't wait for our next adventure!

Special thanks to the Thursday writer's group who welcomed me with open arms and honest feedback. You offered me an education and a sense of community for which I am grateful. I am so glad we went online and continued in a virtual format in the face of the pandemic.

It is also important that I thank Morgan Williams for his perspective and editing. I admire his ability to take a good scene and point out ways that I can make it better.

Sincere thanks go to Matt Witt, my multitalented son, who created the cover for this book. Even as a child, he had an eye for color and design, and it was a special pleasure to see him take my input and create something far beyond what I imagined.

DESIGNER BABIES

Volume Two
Growing Pains

CHAPTER ONE

Larry Knewell readied himself for the tenth visit of at least one of the world's first three designer babies on *Rare Air,* his show on the twenty-four-hour cable channel, CBN. This time was special as it marked the fifth birthday of Adam Clayborn, the very first genetically modified human. While he turned five years old chronologically, he stood six-foot three with broad shoulders and a confident smile. Joining him on the guest sofa was Madeline Blaze and Ensley Springer. They were the second and third gene edited children, born just days later. As with Adam, they too had been genetically altered to mature rapidly, and to all appearances looked to be about twenty-five. To say the world had changed in the five years since their births would be like saying the Grand Canyon is just another ditch.

Larry had been the unofficial mainstream media chronicler of their brief lives and relished his high-profile role. His show thrived at the intersection of politics, science and celebrity and this story had topped all three categories since it burst on the scene. When the program was at its best it was both informative and sensational, and tonight, he couldn't wait to get started. "Happy birthday, Adam, and welcome back to *Rare Air.* What's life like for someone whose birth certificate says they're five years old, but looks and acts like they're a young adult?"

He seemed a perfect blend of his parents with the tawny hair and olive skin of his mother, and blue eyes and solid build of his father. The easy laugh that had been a marker of Adam's even-tempered personality preceded his answer. "It's been eventful, that's for sure. Lately, I've been busy starting a bank for micro businesses around the globe. I think we've done a lot of good."

"We'll come back to discuss your success, but first, let's reintroduce everyone." Larry now looked to Madeline. "Congratulations to you, Madeline, on the success of the *Loud and Proud* tour. I understand you broke a few of your mother's records."

"It's not a competition or anything, but yeah. My fans showed out for me around the world." She was undeniably Gwen Blaze's daughter with the same milky white skin and smile that could light a stadium. Her decision to dye her natural brunette hair lemon yellow was a page straight from her mother's playbook. But she wasn't a copy, as she stood a half-foot taller with jade green eyes instead of sapphire blues. Most controversial was the bigger bust size, which Gwen had insisted be tweaked into her genes.

Larry looked to Maddy's left for the final introduction of the trio. "Ensley Springer is the youngest of this amazing group. Like Adam and Madeline, Ensley is only five calendar years old but has already accomplished so much. I believe you are the youngest graduate of UC Berkley, is that correct?"

"It's good to see you again Larry, and yes, you are correct. Same goes for youngest to earn my PhD in Social Policy. I'm proud to be one of the faces of the GM movement representing the millions of genetically modified children who have followed us three. I believe our life journeys have paved the way for their acceptance in society."

"Let's stay with you for a moment, Ensley. Since your births were announced, there have been approximately ten million additional GM children born, although most without this accelerated maturation edit." Larry's brow furrowed, ready to really get the interview going. "It's not been all roses and sunshine, has it?"

With the confidence of a seasoned politician Ensley responded, flipping her straight silky black hair back, just like her mother. "Every major scientific advancement has bumps in the road and this one is no different. I like to begin any conversation about this subject with an undeniable fact. The birth defect rate in GM babies has been zero-point-five percent while the percentage for natural born children in the same time period has been about three percent. That translates into tens of thousands fewer children having to overcome debilitating impacts to their lives, not to mention all of the diseases we will never develop over our lifetimes. That alone is going to change human health, and the cost of healthcare, in a way government programs or private insurance never could."

While this was true, Larry really wanted to get into the controversial aspects of the Designer Baby movement. After all, conflict and drama drive ratings. "Fair enough, but speak to some of the biggest hurdles you and the others face. Let's start with the World Against Genetic Engineering, WAGE for short. They don't see things the same way as you, do they?"

The mention of the organization founded by Becky Brown and Kelley Slaughter seemed to rattle Ensley's composure. "The world rarely agrees on anything completely, and *that* group certainly disagrees with my views."

Larry pushed, trying to trigger a bigger reaction. "What do you think of the law they've already passed raising income taxes on GM people and the one they're pushing now to exclude GM students from scholarships at public universities? They say that with the boost to your intelligence, GM youth have built in unfair advantages over most other students. Why benefit you even more by taking educational funds away from those who now need them even more to compete with people like you?"

Ensley's smile disappeared, but it seemed she maintained her cool... mostly. "That is disappointing. While we're different in some ways we're still fully human, twenty-three chromosomes, just like everyone else." She paused, then looked him square in the eye. "It reminds me of the racist views of some from our past, like the 'one-drop rule' that became law in many states. It codified that if a person had even one drop of African-American blood, that person was legally considered black. With that designation they were condemned to the degrading segregation of the time. That meant sub-standard schools, restrictions on which neighborhoods they could live, and it put some occupations totally out of reach. We look back on those segregationist tactics as abhorrent, and someday I predict we'll do the same with these efforts."

That was the spark Larry wanted. "Ensley, we could talk about this subject for the entire show, but people also want to hear about other aspects of the lives of the three of you." Now he transitioned back to Madeline, to see if he could do the same with her. "Madeline, as I mentioned, your recent tour topped a few of your mother's attendance records. It's one thing to get the boost to your career by being the child of a celebrity, but it's something else altogether to genetically ensure that you had a terrific singing voice." He paused. "And I'll say this as diplomatically as possible. Your genes were edited with physical enhancements that make you more attractive to members of the opposite sex. Did you really have to work as hard for your success as your mother?"

She seemed to have inherited Gwen's temperament as well. "Mom likes you, but I saw the playback of the time she called you a blowhard and said that you could kiss her ass." A snarky grin inched onto her face. "That's the way I feel about that question. I am who I am, and I put it all out there in my recordings and shows, and people seem to like it… a lot." Her upper lip now raised in a snarl and she thrust her chest toward him. "Any other questions about my music, or would you rather talk about my boobs?"

Larry was simultaneously embarrassed and thrilled. This clip would go viral before he could wrap the segment, and he believed there was no such thing as bad publicity. "No… I think you made your point quite well. Please be sure to give your mother my best regards, and let her know I look forward to having her back again soon."

Madeline's snarl transformed into a smirk, as if proud of the way she handled the situation. "She really does like you, and I'm sure she'll welcome the chance to add to her record number of visits to your show."

With that, Larry turned to Adam for one last set of questions, wanting to get one more moment for this anniversary segment of the show. "Congratulations on your business success, Adam. Having wealthy parents always gives the next generation a head start, but enhanced intelligence certainly must have also played a part. Is that really fair to the rest of us? Isn't this elitist inequality in its highest form?"

The smile on Adam's face never changed. "Larry, have you ever been someone else?"

The question surprised him. "Uh... no. What are you getting at?"

"It's the same for me. This is how I was born, the only person I've ever been. I can't go backwards in time and change my unusual birth, nor can anyone else. What I can do is take the lessons my parents tried to impart to me, as well as the opportunities I've had, and do something that makes a difference. I know I'm fortunate to have two successful parents. As you know, my mother is a leader in the field of sustainability and my father is a key figure in the banking world."

Larry interrupted. "I think your father was on the short list to be Secretary of the Treasury a year or so ago, right?"

"Like I said, he's a key figure, and I guess I inherited some of my interests from both. Micro businesses are located in some of the poorest places on our planet, like sub-Saharan Africa and indigenous regions of South America. The bank I created caters to those kinds of businesses, helping millions of small entrepreneurs raise their standard of living and lifting them out of poverty. I like to think that's helping those that need it the most, and the fact that it's been very successful will allow me to do more in the future. I can't help the circumstances of my birth. I just try to lead a life that makes a difference for others."

Time was running out in this segment and Larry wanted to get the last word. "On the first visit of these three young people to *Rare Air* almost five years ago, we all knew that the world had changed, that rules in place for millennia had forever been broken. In this short conversation we've barely scratched the surface of what our future as a species will look like in the coming years. Will we look back and wonder why we worried so much, or wonder why we didn't address these issues more directly? It's impossible to see what will come next, but what you can be sure of is that until the world reaches consensus, we'll be here covering the issue from all angles. Stay tuned as we next hear from other parents who have followed the path blazed by these young people, as well as from activists who continue the fight against genetic modification of humans. It promises to be another exciting episode of *Rare Air*.

With the wrap of their segment on the show, the three made their way off set. While their lives had been intertwined since birth, it had been at least six months since they had seen each other. Adam enjoyed his work, but sometimes felt as if the world expected him to always be in suit and tie corporate mode. Tonight, with his lifelong friends, he felt energized and ready to loosen up. "Anyone up for dancing or drinks?"

Despite the public nature of her battle with opioid addiction and rehab stints, the question was met with an immediate response from Madeline. "Maddy's always ready for a party. You with us Ens?"

While Adam and Maddy had always been the two most likely to go out on the town, Ensley had two loves; battling for genetic equality for all, and dancing. "It's New York City, how about heading to Chalky's?"

This was exactly what Adam wanted to hear. "Yes! The one place in town where we can dance and hang with people like us."

CHAPTER TWO

Becky Brown caught herself staring at her image on the screen as she waited for the virtual board meeting of WAGE to begin. Her prematurely gray hair styled in a butch faux-hawk cut visually represented the biggest change to her life since the demise of the Reformed branch of the Tree of Life Society. That night her father, Ben Brown, former director of the society, was gunned down for his role in trying to end the threat of GM humans. He had orchestrated multiple unsuccessful attempts to kill all three of the original mothers and their soon-to-be born children, and the retaliation from the Original branch was swift and final. It was the triggering event in the freefall of her life for a few years, as she struggled with the decision to come out as gay while grieving her loss.

Kelley Slaughter joined her at the desk as the clock counted down the final seconds before the virtual meeting began. Her father, Ezra Slaughter, had also been killed that night, but somehow, she had dealt with the loss better. She kissed Becky on the cheek before the shared screen began filling with other leaders of the movement from around the world. "I know that look. You're lost in the past again."

A melancholy smile signaled Becky's return to the here and now, taking in the sweet vision of her wife. Seeing her auburn hair in pigtails with rainbow bands turned her smile closer to full. "Have I told you lately how thankful I am to have you in my life?"

"Almost every day." Kelley's blue-gray eyes smiled back. "You ready to get this show on the road?"

Becky clicked on the 'Begin Meeting' icon, opening all of the windows for attendees from around the planet, then kicked off the weekly session. "Welcome everyone. We look forward to all of your updates on our combined efforts to curb the disastrous effects of those human aberrations. Let's start with an update from South Africa. Lesedi, what's the latest on passage of the "Level Playing Field' legislation?"

The human rights attorney replied forcefully, making her thick accent challenging to understand. "The fear of even more advantages for the rich has mobilized millions and it will almost assuredly pass. The model language we provided made it sail through both houses of parliament and should be signed by the president later this week. I'm so proud of what we're doing to protect what it means to be human."

Nods and verbal agreement channeled in from every corner of the globe until Becky brought the group back to order. The impassioned speech of Lesedi had reminded her of her father and her anger returned. "Genetic modification has spread more than any of us would like, so we must fight harder. We're working here in the US to get the same kind of legislation passed. Every law enacted, every news story of a ban or disqualification from a normal activity, will make the next woman think twice before adding to their numbers." The release felt good, and she thought of her father. *He would be proud of what I'm doing.*

Lloyd Chesterfield chimed in from London. "We're close to having enough votes to establish the first national list of modified humans. It will function similar to a sex offender list, letting anyone go online and get the true status of someone who might be trying to hide their alterations."

"Excellent! We'll shine the light on all who try to conceal their unnatural advantages."

Reports and updates from other members rolled in. Kelley took the lead as the meeting turned to mundane subjects, like budgets and fundraising. After an hour, the meeting ended as

Kelley disconnected them from the network, then leaned back. "We're finished with *that* business."

A long exhale signaled Becky's relief, but the tedious aspects of running an organization of this size always bored her to tears. Kelley's accountant background and willingness to take the lead in these areas was just another reason she loved her so. "With that behind us, we can get on with our *real* priority. Are we set for tonight?"

Glancing at her phone, Kelley saw two messages that read, 'RAGE Ready.' "Phillip and Anfernee just confirmed, that makes ten. We're a go for our raid on Chalky's tonight."

Just reading the word RAGE brought goosebumps to Becky's arms, making her as excited as a kid on Christmas Eve. This was the secret side of the larger WAGE organization, whose sole reason for existence was to terrorize and harass GM people in an up-close and personal way. "This is the part that would *really* make my father proud. Time to crack some skulls. Do you want the baseball bat or crowbar tonight?"

CHAPTER THREE

The beats of electronic dance music were as much felt as heard when Adam, Ensley and Maddy stepped into the dimly lit Chalky's Wild World. It was a key component of the vibe, which helped make it one of their favorite places in the city. Neon lights around the bar and dance floor pulsed to the thumping bassline in dayglow colors that could never be found in nature, while fashionable or funky dressed young people moved and grooved to the pounding rhythms. Kiss Me Kimee, a hostess with electric blue hair and fluorescent lime green make-up, showed the trio to a table in the second tier VIP section. Adam spotted a familiar figure in the DJ booth. "Hell yeah, Yori's on the turntables. It should be an awesome night."

Yori Kobayashi's father wanted his son to be the most accomplished pianist in the world so he paid a genetic bioengineer a million dollars to edit his son's genome to have six fingers on each hand. It turned out that also made him a terrific professional video game player and his musical interest pulled him to follow a DJ career instead of the piano. He flashed a two finger V sign toward the trio and spun the dance version of Maddy's latest hit, *You See Me, I See You*.

Kiss Me Kimee returned, setting a tray of complementary drinks on the table, then without warning, leaned in and kissed Maddy on the lips. She spoke nervously. "I can't believe I just did that, and I hope you don't mind, it's just that I love your song so much! It speaks to the freak in me. I'm so excited to meet you I'm about to pee my pants."

While Adam and Ensley seemed shocked, Maddy barely reacted.

"I get that a lot." She smiled at the obviously smitten hostess and sang along with the girl as her song hit the chorus. "You see me, I see you. You see my freak flag flying, and I see yours too."

It looked like Kimee might explode as her hands gyrated before finally forming a few words. "My god, you're as cool as they say." Her legs pumped up and down without going anywhere. "Maybe I'll see you on the dance floor later?"

"Sure, Kimee. Now go tell Chalky we appreciate the drinks."

Laughing, Adam took one of the beverages from the tray. "I'd forgotten how different your life is from mine. Not a single client has ever kissed me, no matter how much they appreciate the loan I gave them."

Ensley grabbed a cocktail for herself. "Same here. I work on behalf of all kinds of GM kids, but nothing like that has ever happened. Was it like that on the entire tour?"

She was about to answer when Chalky walked up to the table. "So good to see you guys! I wish I knew you were stopping by, we'd have done something really special." His real name was Adimu Juma, but everyone called him Chalky because of his pale skin and white hair. His family had fled Tanzania when he was a child because of fear that superstitious tribesmen might kill him due to his albinism.

"It's been a while since we've hung out, and there's no better place than here, for people like us," said Adam over the increasingly loud music. "We're ready to party, dance and swap stories about our weird lives. In other words, we just want to chill, like normal people."

Chalky spun the remaining open chair around and straddled it, his arms crossed on the back. "Well, you better enjoy your chill now, because even a normal Friday night will get crazy with Yori as the DJ. That boy can make a crowd move, and when word gets out that you three are here? Let's just say this night might start chill, but I can almost guarantee it won't end that way."

CHAPTER FOUR

Becky waited with Kelley and seven others in a plain white cargo van while Phillip did a surveillance run through Chalky's. They hadn't done a raid on the place in almost a year and she was hoping the club's security had eased back to normal levels in the intervening months. Recalling that night made her smile. With mostly the same crew as assembled tonight, the RAGE Raiders, as they called themselves, had sown seeds of fear in the growing modified human community. Their marauding dash through the building had resulted in twenty of those they considered abominations to be hospitalized, and caused over fifty thousand dollars in damages.

The sliding door opened and Phillip hopped into the van, beads of sweat on his forehead, words tumbling out in a torrent. "You're not going to believe who's in there! I mean it's crazy and packed to the beams, a freak show on steroids!"

"Slow down, cowboy." Turning from the driver seat, Becky questioned. "Start from the beginning. What's going on?"

Catching his breath, Phillip began his debrief. "It's insane." He glanced around the darkened interior of the cargo van, looking like he had seen a space alien. "The first three are there, partying like it's New Year's Eve. The joint is jumping."

"The first three? No shit?" Becky replied in amazement as her mind immediately went to the father she never felt able to please. "I've dreamed of a night like this for a long time, finally a chance for some payback."

The news seemed to generate a different reaction in Kelley. "Then security must be through the roof, right? I want revenge, but I'm not down for a suicide mission."

Phillip's face brightened, making his carrot-orange hair stand out even more. "You would think, right? There are two bouncers at the door and a few guards around the perimeter of the dancefloor, but I only counted six, total. If we do this right, I think we can be in and out before they know what hit them."

Becky could barely contain her excitement. "We may never get another chance like this. I say we go. Who's with me?"

It didn't take long to get a unanimous decision, even with Kelley being the last one to raise her hand. They had a standard plan of attack for these terror runs and Becky quickly reviewed their roles. "Agnes and Ian, you good with taking on the bouncers?"

They answered in unison. "Yep."

"Good. The rest of us do as much damage as we can before the guards figure out what's going on. By then they'll be dealing with the stampede of Freakers crawling over each other trying to get out of there. Any questions?"

Cato spoke up. "And if we get lucky enough to spot one of those three, do we treat them any differently?"

Picking up her crowbar and rapping her free palm, Becky replied. "If it's me, then it only means I swing harder. Any other questions before we gear up?"

The question was met with anxious silence, so the group began adjusting black flak jackets and ballistic helmets with tinted shields. Becky could feel the energy building inside the van and it thrilled her. "Hand to the middle, everyone." Each team member extended a gloved hand toward the center of an informal circle as Becky continued. "We're in fast, hit hard, then get out clean. Right?"

A chorus of yeses met her question. "We're doing this on three. One-two-three!"

Together the cheer of "Rage Raiders!" rang inside the van as Phillip slid the door open to begin the assault.

Word spread quickly on the underground Freaker network that Adam, Ensley and Madeline were at Chalky's, resulting in a scene of controlled frenzy and admiration. As the first Designer Babies, they were trailblazers and heroes to all the GM children that followed. They had also become stars to those like Kiss Me Kimee, who were just different. Laser lights flashed to the hypnotic and psychedelic beats being laid down by Yori as the three danced with each other at the center of the crowded floor. Adam shouted to no one in particular. "God, I love this place!" That's when pandemonium broke out as a fire alarm was pulled.

With his perch above the floor, Yori seemed to be the first to realize what was going on. "It's a raid! It's a raid!"

Screams rang out in the manufactured fog on the floor, the red, green and blue laser lights still flashing, creating a surrealistic horror film like setting. Ensley called to Adam and Maddy. "Triangle!"

While none of them had been told anything about the Tree of Life Society, Ensley and Adam had followed in their parents and grandparents' footsteps by training in the martial arts with Master Fong in China. Maddy had begged her mom to join them, thus they all knew to form a triangle facing outward, ready to fend off an attack from any direction. Adam was the first to see the crowbar wielding attacker headed their way. "Here we go!"

He pivoted and kicked, catching the riot gear clad attacker in the mid-section, but not before the iron weapon came crashing toward his head. It connected hard as lights flashed in his eyes, a single syllable escaping his lips as he fell to the ground. "Ooff."

All about them screams and shouts filled the air with panic as Ensley spun around, seeing Adam's attacker holding their left side, a bloody crowbar in hand. Before they could swing again

Ensley launched a counter attack with a flurry of punches landing on the assailant's protected body. A final leg sweep brought the perpetrator to the ground. Ens moved in, pushing away the tinted face shield, then delivering a punishing blow to their nose.

A loud whistle sounded and she heard Maddy cursing as she fought. "You sons of bitches picked the wrong girl to fuck with!"

The sound of the whistle seemed to act as a signal to the attackers who began a coordinated sprint for the back exit. Rather than finish off the assailant she tackled, Ensley rushed to Adam who lay sprawled on the ground. "Adam! Adam! Are you okay! You've got to be okay!"

Kelley heard Phillip's whistle and headed for the backdoor per protocol, stopping when she saw Becky laying still on the dance floor. The adrenaline already flowing through her body felt like it doubled as she feared the worst. She blew two short bursts as a call for help and Cato ran up beside her. She pleaded with her unconscious wife. "You better be okay!" Together they lifted Becky's limp body between them as they moved as fast as they could out of the building, her helmet briefly falling to the ground, before being put back in place by Kelley. "Can't leave any evidence."

Their breathing was labored by the time they reached the van two blocks away. Quickly loading Becky's crumpled figure through the double rear doors. Kelley ran to the driver's seat and hauled ass away from the scene. She called out in panic. "Get that gear off of her and give me an update! How is she?"

Phillip opened a first aid kit then snapped an ammonia inhalant, waving it under Becky's nose. A groan gave their first reassurance before she was able to slur a few words. "Shit. What the hell happened?"

Cato answered as Kelley continued the getaway. "She's awake, but there's already swelling and bruising of her face. We need to get her to a hospital."

Becky resisted, speaking low but steady. "No hospital. Just get me home and we'll figure it out."

Speaking as she drove, Kelley called back, worry and concern coating her words. "How are you feeling, dear?"

Laying still on the floor of the moving vehicle, Becky spoke a little louder and clearer. "Like hell… but I think I gave as good as I got. It felt really good to take a swing at one of those freaks."

CHAPTER FIVE

A groggy Bree Battle glanced at her phone and answered on the third ring. "Hello... Maddy?" Her mind struggled to figure out why the young woman was calling at this hour. "What's wrong?"

Madeline had lost the best of three rock-paper-scissors challenges, so it had fallen to her to call Adam's parents as their taxi trailed the ambulance. "Mrs. Battle, uh... there's been an incident and Adam's hurt. He's on his way to the hospital."

"Wait, what...what happened?" Bree bolted upright, swinging her legs over the side of the bed, suddenly thrust from peaceful sleep to wide awake. "Tell me he's okay!"

Maddy's voice shook. "The EMT's said his vitals were stable as they put him in the ambulance. We're headed to Mount Sinai Beth Israel."

Bree leaned over and shook Ansen. "Wake up! Something's happened to Adam. We have to go to the hospital!" As he startled, Bree turned back to the phone conversation. "What happened? Are you alright?"

Glancing toward Ensley, Maddy answered for both. "Ens and I are a little shaken, but we're okay. We were all just hanging out at Chalky's when some people burst in swinging bats and clubs. We fought back, but one of them hit Adam in the head."

"Oh my God! We'll be there as soon as we can." She thought for a moment, then added, "have you two called your mothers? You better do that before they find out on Twitter."

Maddy released a tense breath. "We wanted to talk to you first, but those are our next calls. We're pulling into the hospital, so we'll see you when you get here."

"Thanks for calling and I'm so glad you and Ensley are alright. We'll be there soon." Hanging up, Bree turned to Ansen, who had already returned from the closet with pants and a fresh white button-down shirt. "I need to call Dr. Chavez. Adam's physiology isn't exactly normal and she'll know what to do."

He shoved one leg after another into his khaki trousers, his voice tinged with frustration. "I wish we had kept a body guard with him for a little longer. We could have prevented this."

Bree shed her nightgown and pulled a floral print dress over her head, getting ready as fast as she could. "Could have... should have. We'll talk about all of that after we find out how he's doing. Right now, that's all I can think about." As they traveled to be by Adam's side, an old familiar string of thought crept back. *The hyper driven life those three have been handed is not fair to them, or us. I mean, just three years ago they were in middle school for Christ's sake.*

After a quick trip to the hospital, they found Ensley and Madeline in an emergency department waiting room filled with a normal Friday night cultural cross section of New Yorkers. Bree hugged both of the young women. "I'm so glad you two are safe."

An announcement came over the intercom. "Will the family of Adam Clayborn please come to consultation room two."

After giving the girls another embrace, Bree took a deep breath and grabbed Ansen's hand. "I'm sure this doctor isn't going to like what we have to say."

Stepping into the small room, they were met by a tall, thin physician with striking red hair pulled back in a short ponytail. Bree detected a Russian accent as the woman spoke. "Hello, I'm Dr. Katarina Rostov, and I'm sorry that we're meeting under these circumstances. I've followed your story with interest these past few years."

Anxious, Bree pushed. "How's our son? Please tell us he's alright."

"He's awake and resting comfortably, lucky to be alive. If the blow to his head had landed just a few inches to the left it could have killed him."

Ansen pulled Bree close as she shed a few tears. He now spoke to the physician. "That's certainly good news. Does that mean he's okay?"

The doctor's freckled forehead crinkled. "He's not out of the woods yet. He sustained a straight-line fracture of his skull and we've stitched up a five-inch gash in his scalp. We'll be moving him up to one of the floors for observation, just in case. Serious complications sometimes manifest a few hours after this kind of trauma."

Wiping her cheek, Bree stopped the physician. "No, we're taking him home."

The doctor looked flabbergasted as her jaw dropped. "Do you understand what I'm saying? Your son sustained a major head injury. If a blood clot develops and he doesn't receive immediate medical attention, he will die. That's not speculation, Mrs. Battle, that's a certainty."

Bree's golden eyes hardened as her mind replayed Dr. Chavez's words from their brief phone call. *There are things those doctors don't need to see. Get him out of the hospital, and I'll be there by morning. Trust me when I say he'll be fine, that his life will only be in danger if he stays there.* Bree knew exactly what she meant, so her blunt response carried the air of finality. "I said we're taking him home. Now, get the paperwork ready because we're leaving."

Taking a step back, Dr. Rostov folded her arms. "I guess everything I've heard about you is true. You really do think you can play God."

Bree raised her hand and pointed for emphasis as she took a

step toward the doctor, her voice low and growling. "You know nothing about me or my son. Take me to him, then do what you need to do, because we'll be out of here in fifteen minutes. Am I clear?"

The doctor sneered. "Now I understand why so many are against what you've done. You think the regular rules and the laws of nature don't apply to you. I still don't know how you got a five-year-old declared a legal adult." She began walking away, then stopped and turned, symbolically wiping her hands. "I hope you do know something I don't, because if anything happens to that young man, his blood will be on your hands, not mine." Her eyes seemed to plead for Bree to change her mind and when no reply came, her shoulders sagged. "Follow me and we'll get you and your son on your way... against all medical advice."

Phillip returned to Becky and Kelley's apartment after stashing the van in a warehouse used by the business he inherited following his father's suicide. He rejoined the rest of the RAGE crew as Kelley and Anfernee tended to Becky. Kelley held her hand as Anfernee gently pressed the outside of her swollen nose. He pronounced the obvious verdict. "Sure enough, it's broken. You really should get a CT just to make sure it's nothing more serious."

Becky lightly touched her nose, wincing once. "Yeah, that's not going to happen. I can't risk showing up at a hospital the same night one of those precious genetic monsters is hurt, it could put us all in *serious* danger. You're an EMT, patch me up and I'll be good as new in no time."

Anfernee retrieved his more complete medical kit from his car and began the process of packing her nose with gauze. "Kelley, get us an ice pack or some ice cubes in a Ziploc bag wrapped in a washcloth. There's not much I can do about those two black eyes, but a cold compress should help with the swelling while I make a run to a pharmacy to get a nasal splint. I know you're not going to the hospital, but you have to promise me you will if you have symptoms other than localized pain. Deal?"

She gave the only answer she could. "Deal."

Anfernee stopped at the door. "And I need you to swear you won't blame me if you end up with a witch's nose."

Her laugh triggered an immediate painful groan. "Son of a bitch, that smarts." Coco, their papillon companion dog rushed to her side. She comforted the pup as well as Anfernee. "Don't worry, most people think I look that way already, so they wouldn't even notice." She rubbed Coco's ears." Now, hurry up and get back so we can swap stories. I want to hear all about how we served notice to those Freakers tonight."

CHAPTER SIX

Bree had checked in on Adam at least a dozen times during the night, each time quietly entering his childhood bedroom. Every time she heard his rhythmic breathing, her fear ebbed a little, like a receding tide. By morning, she was exhausted while he rested as if nothing at all had happened. She stirred French vanilla creamer in her coffee as morning light hit their Upper East Side residence. *I guess I'll always worry about him.*

Ansen rubbed his eyes as he entered the kitchen in a tee-shirt and pajama pants. "That coffee sure smells good." He grabbed a cup from a cabinet and popped in a Keurig pod, checking in with her as he waited for his caffeine fix to brew. "How did he sleep last night?"

"Like a baby, as far as I could tell. His breathing seemed normal and he rolled over a couple of times."

With the coffee maker completing its cycle, he picked up the cup and blew over the onyx black surface before taking his first sip. "And how about you? Did you get any sleep?"

She was about to answer when the doorbell rang. "She's right on time." While Bree had long ago reconciled her early distrust of Dr. Chavez because of the love she felt for Adam, their relationship had never moved past respect, into friendship. "And for once, I'm glad she's here."

When Bree opened the door, the woman who had led the world into the reality of genetic modified humans, walked in as if she owned the place. "I smell coffee. I take mine black, with one sugar please."

Bree shot Ansen a knowing glance as the direct woman, dressed in her customary black scrubs, made herself at home at the massive kitchen island. Bree joined her, speaking sincerely. "I appreciate you coming on such short notice. Even knowing all we know about his physiology, I was really scared last night. If you'll recall, I had a lot of mixed feelings during my unusual pregnancy, and there's no way I could have imagined how much I love this child. I would have been crushed if ..." She couldn't finish the awful sentence, her head bowed, resting in her hands.

Ansen slid Dr. Chavez her coffee as Adam entered, his bandaged head making him look like a mummy that had awoken and not quite escaped all of his wrapping. He joked. "Who's making all the racket out here while some of us are trying to sleep?"

"How is my favorite patient?" The doctor's trademark crooked smile widened. "I hear you gave your parents quite the scare last night."

He blushed. "Yeah, that wasn't my intention when the evening started. I can promise you I wasn't looking for trouble, but it sure found us." Adam looked over at his father. "Hey, dad. I'm starved. Could I get some breakfast?"

Dr. Chavez nodded. "All is as I expected. Let's enjoy some food, then I'll do an exam. How does that sound?"

Taking the seat beside his mother, Adam agreed. "Pancakes, with bacon and eggs?"

"That does sound good." Bree laughed softly, remembering how hungry she had been during her sped-up pregnancy. "Want some help, Hon?"

Ansen was already putting pans on burners. "You had sentry duty last night, so I'll handle cooking duties." He winked at Bree. "That way you can all catch up with each other."

Leaning on the quartz island surface, Bree remembered the deal she had struck with Dr. Chavez a little over five years ago. Agree to carry the first GM human in return for curing her incurable brain cancer. She had been bitter about the perceived blackmail of the situation, and could never have dreamed she would be sitting so comfortably together these few years later, yet here they were. "So, how is the Designer Baby business these days?"

"Business is booming, just as I expected. And it's all thanks to you and this fine young man." Dr. Chavez looked at Bree and Adam, speaking with a softness rarely heard from her. "You've all been outstanding role models to the parents and children who have followed in your footsteps." The tender moment didn't last long as she spoke harshly, her true personality re-emerging. "Now, if the world would knock some sense into those WAGE people things would be even better."

Adam knew nothing of the Tree of Life Society that had worked toward his birth for centuries, but as members, Bree and Ansen certainly did. They heard her words as she probably intended, a call to action to retaliate for the violence directed at Adam. Ansen smiled innocently. "I'm sure they'll get what's coming to them, but right now let's eat. Breakfast is almost ready."

After a leisurely meal where Adam's latest business venture and appearance on television last night were the primary topics, it was time for his exam. Pulling a dining room chair near the large window provided the lighting Dr. Chavez requested. "Have a seat, young man, and let's take a look." She gently removed the wrap from his head, then used a damp washcloth to clean the little bit of dried blood that remained from the cleaning of the wound last night. "Just as I suspected." She motioned to Bree. "Take a look, mom."

The doctor's casual tone told Bree exactly what she knew she would see as she leaned closer. "Not even a small scar. A five-inch gash healed overnight." She sighed. "I'm still glad we called you."

Adam spoke brightly before Dr. Chavez could reply. "Just like always. I don't know why you two worry so much."

Both women laughed, then Bree answered her son. "It's a mom's job to worry at least a little, and you've never had a wound like this before. Besides, even with the skin healing so quickly, there is a skull fracture still to consider."

Standing, he looked at both of them with a cocky grin. "You two have any doubt that's not healed as well?"

A wink from Dr. Chavez signaled her attitude. "Confidence is good, Adam, but arrogance will get you killed. You have been blessed with remarkable physical traits, but you're not invincible. Always be bold, but never be stupid. Understand?"

His cocky grin was now replaced by a charismatic smile. "I'm just messing with you guys, I know the rules. I'll get my head rewrapped as a disguise before I go anywhere. We can't have people thinking I'm some kind of super human." He hugged each of them, then headed for his room. "I'll text Ens and Maddy and let them know I'm okay. I bet they're at least a little worried."

Bree looked at Dr. Chavez with a bemused headshake. "Was this what you were thinking when you made those gene edits?"

"The rapid self-healing, yes." The doctor crossed her arms. "The cocky attitude, not so much. You and Ansen have done a wonderful job raising this special young man, and he seems to be thriving."

Bree interjected. "I sense a 'but' coming."

Dr. Chavez reached for Bree's arm. "We're in uncharted water here. He has the body and mind of a full-grown man - with only five years of life experience. He's the smartest one in this apartment, but also the one most likely to do something stupid because of his sheer youth. This is a very dangerous time for everyone."

Ansen had listened from the kitchen and now joined them, putting his arm around his wife's shoulders. "I know we'll get through these next few years together, but there are things that need our attention right now." He lowered his voice. "I received a text a few minutes ago. We're having a council meeting later today to address what happened last night. The society can't stand idly by when these first three children are attacked. Whoever did this must pay for what they've done."

A shiver ran through Bree as she remembered the night Adam was born. The radical Reformed splinter group of the Tree of Life Society had tried to kill her and Ansen, as well as the parents of Ensley and Maddy. The massive military style raid failed, triggering a bloody reprisal that killed several of the rouge leaders and brought most of the remaining rebel elements back into the larger fellowship. "The thought of another group taking up arms against us just because we represent something new makes me sick. I know we must send a message, but promise me you'll use violence as a last resort."

"You know Kristoff." Ansen invoked the name of the patriarch of the society. "He sees the use of force to make a point as sometimes necessary, but ultimately a failure of imagination." He sighed. "Speaking of imagination, it's hard for me to believe it's time to discuss when and how we're going to have the conversation with Adam about his society heritage."

"Another reason I chose to never have children."

The snarky remark from Dr. Chavez brought a subdued laugh from Bree. "So instead, you genetically edited Adam and Ensley, forcing us to figure this out at warp speed. Thanks a lot. Ansen's parents had twenty-seven years, and I didn't find out until I was almost thirty." Her words turned frosty. "Just another example of how Adam is being forced to grow up way too fast."

The doctor cackled at Bree's retort. "Ah, the joys of parenthood. Now, if you two love birds will excuse me, I have important society business to attend while I'm here. If anything changes with the boy's condition, give me a call, otherwise I'll check in before I head back to Prague." She walked away and stuck her head in Adam's room to say goodbye, then waved as she exited the apartment. "Ciao."

Bree and Ansen stood alone as she turned to him. "Do you think she'll take a plane to Prague, or just hop on her broom?"

CHAPTER SEVEN

Morning sun cascaded through the large windows of the Hell's Kitchen apartment shared by Kelley and Becky. Becky began stirring, so Kelley quickly went to the kitchen and brought back a cup of green tea and two acetaminophen tablets to her girl. "How are you feeling, dear?"

"Like I was in a bar fight last night." Becky gingerly touched her nose. "Ouch, guess that wasn't a dream." She took the cup and saucer and chased the tablets with the warm liquid, her thoughts wondering back to the raid at Chalky's. "My god, that was so much fun."

"You call that fun? Try mixing adrenaline with terror, then spinning the concoction in a blender. For a moment I thought I lost you, and just recalling it makes me ill all over again."

Becky caressed Kelley's cheek with feathery strokes. "A pure soul with a heart of gold. I'm the luckiest woman in the world." Becky's words had the intended effect as Kelley cuddled close, nestling under her protective reach. "And what could make that kind of woman happier?"

A cherubic smile plumped Kelley's cheeks. "A baby of our own."

A downhearted sigh met the comment. "I wish our fathers could have lived to see this day." She paused. "But that damned society and their support of genetic tyranny made sure that didn't happen."

"True, but to be fair, our reformed group wasn't too keen on our kind of love either. I miss my father too, but I'm not sure you would have ever come out if that branch of the society hadn't ended." She took Becky's hand. "I love you so much it lessens the sting of our losses."

Her soft words were spoken with such tenderness that Becky's eyes moistened, but she refused to give in to actual tears, using humor to deflect the depths of her feelings. "Dr. Simon's might have some questions about the stability of our relationship when she sees me with these two shiners. Are you ready to play the tough girl today and set her straight?"

"Shut up!" Kelley poked Becky's ribs hard and laughed. "Don't be joking like that. Our appointment is at two, and we really do have to come up with some kind of story for how you look." Her jesting turned serious. "It really could be a red flag and delay us from moving forward with invitro, and that would break my heart."

"Now, now. We won't let that happen." Her mind raced, trying to think up a believable cover story. "I know. We'll tell her things got heated in my karate class. It's not like that's never happened, right?"

"But you're always the one delivering the punishment, not receiving it."

Becky closed her eyes and smiled, replaying the encounter with Adam in her mind, remembering his crumpled bleeding body on the floor, before getting knocked out herself. "I'll tell her some of the truth. I'll say, 'Doctor Simon, if you think this is bad, you should see the other guy."

CHAPTER EIGHT

Adam had listened to his overprotective mother all morning, itching to get out of the house and see his friends. The unnecessary head bandage was an irritation both figuratively and literally, but he understood the reason and grudgingly complied with the decision. "Bye mom. Don't wait on me for dinner, I might go back to my place tonight." He bolted from the apartment as soon as his Uber ride arrived, heading straight to Chalky's to meet up with Ensley and Madeline.

The police tape across the door was a bright yellow reminder of the previous night's happenings. He exited the car, gave the driver a five-star rating and a fifteen percent tip, then raised the tape enough to walk under. Inside, a crew was at work sweeping broken glass and splinters of barstools. "Damn, they sure made a mess of the place."

Chalky's slightly accented voice boomed. "Over here!"

Turning, he spotted Chalky, Maddy and Ensley seated at a corner table. He glided over, feigning a wobble as he got close. "Anyone else hear a strange ringing sound?"

Maddy rose and delivered a playful fist to his shoulder, just a little too hard. "You better be glad you're okay, otherwise I would have to hurt you."

"Ouch." He joked. "Good to see you, too."

Ensley stood and took the opposite approach, grabbing him in a bear hug, squeezing tight. "There was so much blood on the floor." She hugged again, then went up on tiptoes to kiss his cheek. "I worried about you all night, even after they said you went home."

Even though it was just a peck on the cheek, he blushed and felt warm inside. Lately, he had been thinking about these two women in a different, perhaps romantic light, but had never acted on those thoughts. When various scenarios played in his mind, he thought that if he were to somehow end up in a relationship with either, it would probably be with Ensley, but thinking of Maddy always made him smile, too. He reached for Ensley's hand and for the first time noticed how her dark eyes caught the light. "That means a lot."

Adam reached his other hand toward Maddy, completing the circle that formed the closest relationships in his young life. "Thanks for having my back, both of you, I can't think of anyone else with whom I would want to go into a brawl."

Chalky broke the mood. "Any chance one of you freaks knows how to push a broom. I would like to reopen tonight."

The girls laughed at his choice of words as Adam answered in a serious tone. "Anyone else calls me that and we've got a problem." Now he laughed as well. "Hand me a freakin' broom, you freak."

Instead, Chalky wrapped him in a brief guy hug, then stepped back. "I can't believe you're standing here today. Like Ens said, there was a lot of blood."

Adam nodded, then glanced around at the damage. "How's everyone else?"

Chalky's head dropped slightly. "Some had it rough. A couple of broken bones and a lot of bumps and bruises, but it could have been so much worse. Even with the damage to the place, I feel lucky." His eyes landed on Adam's bandaged head. "You sure it's okay for you to be here?"

"Yeah. Just a scratch." He didn't like lying to Chalky, but it was what he had to do. "They say no heavy lifting for a couple of days, then I'll be good as new.

It seemed to be what Chalky wanted to hear. "That's the best thing I've heard all day. Why don't you guys chill over here while I go talk to the clean-up crew."

He stepped away, leaving the three alone. Ensley broke the silence as they sat. "It was a lot worse than that, wasn't it?"

Adam looked down, unsure if he should tell them the truth, as his parents had drilled in his head that he should keep this a secret from everyone, even his best friends. He decided to hint and see if either of them responded. "You guys know how it is… right?"

Ensley's eyes narrowed. "My parents swore me to secrecy because they weren't sure what edits you guys might have, and I never had a severe injury until last year. I broke my leg skiing and dad refused to take me to the hospital. Mom nearly blew a fuse, while cursing Dr. Chavez for not telling them about the rapid healing edit, then thanking her for doing it anyway. Dad put me in a splint for two days, even though I was fine in only one.

Sighing, Maddy told her story. "Same with my folks. Since dad did my edits, he wasn't sure what traits were altered with you guys, so they demanded total secrecy." A suspicious smile turned upward. "Did you know we can't drown?"

They answered in unison. "What?"

"Yeah. It was before I learned to swim and mom and dad were arguing about something. They totally forgot about me and I fell into the deep end of the pool. I was old enough that I remember my panic when I gasped and water went into my lungs. I tried to scream, but the water muffled the sound. I'm not sure exactly how long I was down there, but my mom came unglued as dad dove in and pulled me out. I coughed up the water, then calmly told them I wanted ice-cream. They gave me the whole carton. We always knew I healed differently, but they weren't sure of the extent of everyone's edits, so they made me swear never to tell."

"Speaking of Chavez, she stopped by to check on me this morning and made a comment about me not being completely invincible. I guess there are limits to our healing abilities, just glad I didn't reach them last night."

That comment seemed to fire Maddy's temper. "Speaking of last night, one of my Twitter followers was here and sent me a private DM this morning. Said she thought she recognized the person who attacked you."

Ensley's jaw set. "How, they had their faces covered."

"Said she's in a karate class with a bitch built like a fireplug who has the same haircut. She got a good look when her helmet fell off. Swears on it. So, I did a deep dive on the dark web and found out some interesting shit."

Adam leaned in as his forehead creased, his thoughts turning to revenge as the day progressed. "Spit it out. What did you find?"

Maddy scanned, appearing to make sure no one was listening, then pointed to Adam and lowered her voice like a spirit telling a secret from beyond the grave. "Her name is Becky Brown, and here's the weird thing. According to news reports, her father was killed in a home invasion … on the night *you* were born."

Adam felt queasy, his eyes widening. "That… that's strange." He drew a sharp breath, trying to stop his mind from running with this odd coincidence. "I'm sure it must be a fluke."

"Really, want to hear something even more bizarre?"

He did, as his thoughts went to a dark place, wondering how far he would go getting payback. Would he go past the time he got in a fistfight on the playground with the bully who pushed him down the stairs, sending him to the hospital and getting himself expelled from school? His mouth opened and words tumbled out like boulders rolling down a hill. "Tell me, tell me everything."

Maddy's eyes were wild and danced between them, as if at a rave. "She has a wife, and guess what?"

Ens played the smart ass. "She's a lesbian?"

Adam always liked Ensley's sense of humor, but Madeline wasn't joking around. "Duh, but that's not what's weird. Want to know what is?"

The answer suddenly flashed in his mind and his words carried the weight of truth. "Her father died the same night, the same way. This wasn't random, we're all connected."

They all leaned back as Maddy made a gesture with her hand exploding from her head. "Mind blown, right?"

Chalky walked back to the group. "Seems pretty intense over here. What's going on?"

A cocked eye and smirking grin from Adam met his question. "We were just about to plan a surprise party for a couple of new acquaintances, one they won't forget."

"Great! How about having it here?"

Adam knew that his answer would be heard one way by Chalky and another by Ens and Maddy. "Us three will hang here tonight to draw a big crowd for you, but the party we're planning needs to be a small, intimate affair. You know, up close and personal. Right girls?"

CHAPTER NINE

Kelley and Becky held hands as they walked into the high-rise building on the Upper West Side. Becky pushed the button for the twentieth floor, then practiced her lie to cover for her black eyes. "Karate practice... you should see the other guy." She bent down and kissed Kelley's cheek. "How's that sound?"

"Fine."

With Kelley's voice a half-step too high and smile a half-size too wide, Becky knew she was super nervous. "Everything is going to go great. We'll hear the news we want, I'm sure."

She gripped Becky's hand tighter. "I hope you're right."

The door opened and they entered the lobby of The Alpha Baby Center, checked in quickly, then sat close together on a cushy leather loveseat. A tech in pink scrubs called out. "Brown and Slaughter?"

After completing yet another questionnaire, their wait was short. Dr. Simon entered with a big smile on her petite face, which then morphed into a blank expression. "What happened to you?"

Becky could feel her cheeks getting hot. "Things got a little out of hand in karate class." She delivered her practiced line with a twinkle in her eye. "You should see my sparring partner."

The practice worked as Dr. Simon gave a small laugh. "Another reason I carry a Taser instead."

A head bob and shoulder shrug sealed the deception. "That works too."

Dr. Simon's grin returned. "I'm pleased to tell you that all of Kelley's tests came back normal. She can begin taking the medication to stimulate her ovaries, and in a couple of weeks we'll harvest several eggs. We'll freeze those we don't use for potential other children, should you want more in the future."

Kelley's eyes spilled tears of happiness as Becky embraced her. Becky answered with choked words. "Thank you, Dr. Simon. This means so much..."

The doctor reached for Becky's shoulder. "And your brother is still willing to be the sperm donor?"

Her head nodded as she wiped her damp eyes, careful to not touch her broken nose. "Yes. He understands it's the only way that this child will be biologically related to both Kelley and myself. I'm sure we would love a child from another sperm donor, but we were both raised in families that put a premium on extending the family line." Her eyes cut to Kelley for a moment at the veiled reference to the society. "And, while our fathers would have a hard time with our marriage, were they still alive, I believe with all my heart they would be thrilled to know this branch of our family will continue."

"It also protects both of you if there were ever to be a custody battle in the future. Your child will carry genes from both your families."

Becky didn't want to talk about anything going wrong, only plan for a happy future together. "Thank you again, Dr. Simon. You're a miracle worker."

Dr. Simon laced her hands together. "I just want to do my part to give you the special child you deserve."

CHAPTER TEN

Ansen closed the door to his study for the four o'clock video conference. One by one, council members from around the globe filled the screen, with Kristoff Svoboda filling the center square. He noted darker circles under the leader's eyes as well as more sag in his jaws. *Age, and the burdens of leadership sure take their toll.*

Kristoff got right to the point. "The stain of the reformers has faded, but refuses to disappear into the ash heap of history. Most peacefully returned to our order, some were eliminated, but a few unrepentant snakes still crawl in dark shadows, striking quickly then scurrying back to their secret dens."

The grumbling was immediate and sustained, until Ansen spoke. "I hope that means you can share with us the identities of those who targeted the first three. It's important for everyone, but it's also personal for me and Zadie."

Sameer Raj spoke from Seattle. "I saw the news saying that Adam left the hospital. I hope that means he's alright."

Even among the council, some aspects of Adam's and Ensley's physiology were kept hidden and now was not the time to reveal this aspect of the young man's genetic enhancements. Ansen swallowed hard as he shaded the truth. "Thankfully, the injuries were not as severe as first thought. He took quite a blow to the head, but should recover with no long-term effects."

Kristoff continued and Ansen sensed the lowering of tension on the call. "While we are all happy he will recover quickly, it does not change the fact that our special children are being targeted, and not just by laws and codified discrimination."

Imka Nkosi joined the conversation from her South African home, her voice indignant. "I've personally felt the jackboot of discrimination and know that the longer it is allowed to persist, the more entrenched it becomes. We must stand up for our future."

A chorus of support poured in from around the globe, finally settling when Kristoff cleared his throat. "As you know, Zadie Springer has been heading our PR campaign to blunt the systemic cultural and legal assault on our special children. I've asked her to provide an update before we discuss other, more direct responses to what happened last night."

After the shared intensity of the night Adam was born, Ansen thought of Zadie more like a sister than just a friend. Her career was thriving now, with a little help from the society, as the owner of the advertising firm where she once worked. She had been invited to join the board as another display of official support for all society women to take the genetic modification route for their next pregnancy. She spoke from her Atlanta home. "Last night the most egregious attack yet on society children occurred, and as with Ansen, it hit close to home."

He noticed for the first time that a few strands of gray hair framed her face and his mind returned to a place it had gone many times before. *For all the discrimination they might endure, due to their genome edits, aging is something our children may not experience for years.*

Zadie's presentation focused his attention. "As you know, Adam, Ensley, and Gwen Blaze's daughter, Madeline were viciously attacked in a Manhattan dance club last night, thankfully with none sustaining critical injuries. The good news is that as we learned five years ago, even when people are against genetic modifications, it doesn't mean that they want to see others savagely attacked. Just ask Gwen Blaze. She rode the reformer's attacks straight to a Grammy."

From Sydney Australia, Charlotte Beckett posed a question. "Is the same thing happening now?"

Nodding, Zadie answered. "Yes. Gwen was all over it this morning on every social media platform, like a protective mother hen. I heard from her just a few minutes ago telling me she's working to get us three first mothers back on *Rare Air,* with Larry Knewell."

Ansen heard Bree's phone ringing somewhere in the house and knew exactly who was calling. *Gwen's on point.*

Zadie continued. "And the apple didn't fall far from the tree. Madeline's social media footprint is almost as big and her fans actually took to the streets this afternoon in a spontaneous march against GM phobia. All the networks are covering it, so while it was a harrowing experience for our children, we'll use it to maximum advantage."

Liza Howard joined the conversation. "This will also help move the dial with some of the politicians we're working. Nothing like voters marching to get their attention. I'll see if Senator Jackson will finally move the Equal Treatment bill out of committee. It's been stalled for too long."

Hearing Liza speak wasn't a shock to Ansen. As a reward for helping mend the schism between the originals and the breakaway reformers, she was given a seat on the council. He knew it was the politically wise thing to do, but she had been the leader of a group that nearly killed them all, and her presence still bothered him. He had worked hard to perfect a neutral expression any time she spoke. "And I'll have lunch with Senator Alfonse this week and see if he'll get on board. We live in the same building, and he knows Adam." Ansen hated to use the attack on his son like this, but the big picture was these kinds of laws were important to keep him safe.

Kristoff nodded. "Excellent. Those efforts are how we win in the long term, but until then we need to send a message that these first three are off limits. While the police are investigating the incident last night, we've taken an even sharper approach. One of our members is strategically placed in the NSA and she's gotten us footage from a surveillance satellite with near constant coverage of New York. The bottom line is we now know the identities of those that harmed Adam." Without warning Kristoff's eyes glanced left. "Please forgive me, but I must take this call. It shouldn't take more than a moment." With that, he muted the videoconference, leaving the council in virtual suspense.

Wonder what that's about? While Ansen waited for Kristoff to return, he looked around at the current configuration of the council, wondering how the long-hinted retirement of the current patriarch would play out. It was a given that Liza would make a play for the job, and that didn't sit right with him. *I just don't trust her.* Then there was the old guard of Imka, Sameer and Charlotte. They had the experience, but he doubted they had the charisma to gain enough votes. That left the young guns like himself, Master Fong, Zadie and the recently added Stephan Svoboda, the youngest son of the current leader. *I just hope there's not too much palace intrigue.* As he looked at the faces again, his thoughts clarified. *Who am I kidding?*

True to his pledge, Kristoff was back quickly, a new bounce in his voice. "I have good news, and a change in plans. We are now in possession of information that could eliminate the threat to our children. Therefore, I am postponing announcing plans for retribution against those we have identified as the perpetrators, in favor of a new plan."

"Always the man of mystery." Sameer's upbeat personality came through in a hardy laugh. "Don't keep us in suspense!"

Kristoff smiled, his mood seeming to lift. "Only in rare circumstances do I ask for your understanding as I keep certain information secret, and this is one of those times."

Imka's voice carried an air of mischief. "I think the last time was shielding us from the true nature of Zadie's pregnancy. That turned out to be the lynchpin that eventually brought down the reformers, ultimately leading to healing our rift."

The mood on the call chilled in an instant, and onscreen Ansen saw Zadie's head bow. *Why did Imka say that?* He spoke in Zadie's defense. "While we rejoice in the reunion, those were dark days for many. Lives were lost and families scarred, including those who serve alongside us today, like Zadie... and Liza."

His point landed as Charlotte concurred. "Ansen's right. We're better when we're united, and reopening old wounds only weaken us." She transitioned. "Kristoff, what *can* you tell us of this new information?"

"Well said, Charlotte." A sly grin crept on Kristoff's face. "We pride ourselves on having imagination in responding to threats, and this time is no different. Right now, anything I share could endanger the plan, so I am asking for your trust, with the promise that if successful we will be able to significantly lower the venomous actions against our children in a non-violent way. Will you trust me again?"

Liza sat taller in her seat. "Kristoff, your wisdom and leadership spared my life, as well as Zadie's. I am thankful for the renewed fellowship of our order, and today we work to build a better future together. You have my trust and my vote in this matter."

She's good, I'll give her that. Ansen could see the nods onscreen and recognized Liza's skill as a politician. "I add my vote in support as well."

A flood of backing flowed in from around the globe, with no dissent for the patriarch's request. Kristoff spoke like the kindly grandfather that he was. "Thank you all for your trust." Then his tenor changed. "Rest assured we will not hesitate to change courses if the new plan fails. Our children are the future and *will* be protected at any cost."

CHAPTER ELEVEN

Ray had listened to Gwen raise her voice over dinner every night this week. Tonight, she was venting about her difficulty memorizing the lyrics for a song on her next record. He knew that irritability and difficulty concentrating were two of the early symptoms of Huntington's Disease, the genes for which they both carried. He held his tongue as his mind went to a place he hated. *God, please don't let this be the beginning. Please. My research isn't far enough along.*

She wasn't finished. "And when is Maddy coming home?"

She's got a lot on her mind right now, maybe it's just stress. "She'll be here Thursday, like we talked about last night."

Her eyes narrowed and forehead wrinkled. "Oh... of course. Now I remember... Thursday."

It didn't look like she remembered, but there was no reason to belabor the point. "Yeah, I'll be glad to see her, too. She acts all grown up, but she's still our little girl."

Gwen's face brightened, the change in subject seeming to have a positive impact on her mood. "I hope she's been working on new material, maybe even another duet for us. We work so well together, almost like sisters, and the last one went platinum."

This was the woman he loved, always charging ahead to the next triumph. "I bet she does. She's always loved singing with you, and maybe she'll even have some time to hang with me in the lab. With all of her creativity, she sometimes sees possibilities I don't."

Her mood swung as fast as a metronome set on a high tempo,

and tears burst forth with no warning. "You're talking about cures, aren't you? Cures you haven't found yet." Her elbows landed heavy on the table, then her head fell into her hands. "It's started hasn't it. My worst nightmare is going to happen. The Huntington's monster is coming for me."

Ray was by her side in an instant, pulling her up in a tight embrace. *Rapid mood swings... another sign.* "Shh, shh. I've made a lot of progress, and so have a lot of other labs. We're going to beat this, I promise." He said the words with conviction because he wanted to speak that future into existence, dreading what their world would look like if he couldn't make it come true.

"I'm scared, Ray, really scared."

He gently stroked her hair, currently platinum blonde with lime green highlights. "I'm right here with you, every step of the way. We'll get through this together, I promise."

"No sugar coating it, how close are you?" She eased her grip and looked up, wet eyes glistening like diamond chandeliers, voice trembling. "Tell me the truth."

"How about we pour a glass of wine and go sit on the patio. We'll watch the waves roll in as the sun sets, while I tell you the latest."

Gwen rubbed her wet eyes while speaking softly. "Sure, okay." She sniffed. "A glass of wine sounds good."

Ray poured two glasses of cabernet, then joined her on the massive stone patio with stunning pacific views. He settled in the chair beside her, hoping but failing to gauge her mood. *Here goes nothing... or everything.* "We've made some real progress, especially in our mouse models. It's very promising."

"Really promising? Really promising like I should walk over to the lab in the morning and get my first treatment, or really promising like ten years after I'm dead you'll be starting human trials?"

The fading daylight and gathering darkness matched his mood as he knew the answer to her question lay somewhere in between, but probably closer to the worst-case scenario. He spun the answer as best he could while still telling the truth. "Science doesn't always advance in a straight line, and you've seen firsthand some of the giant leaps that can happen almost overnight. No one thought Dr. Chavez was close to being able to make so many specific edits to human embryos, but she was. I learned from her, and because of that, Madeline will never have to face the family curse. I believe we can achieve the same kind of breakthrough for Huntington's, and I need you to believe."

She raised her glass, took two long swigs, then set it down gently. "I'll make you a deal. I'll believe, right up until my symptoms get severe, then you have two options." She paused and took another drink. "Option one is to begin whatever treatment you have at that point, even if never tested in a single human. We watched our mothers die, so we both know I'll be willing to take any chance to save myself from that fate."

He knew the other option, but wanted her to say it aloud to judge her will. "And if I won't, because it's too dangerous?"

Gwen finished her wine and spoke calmly. "Then suicide is my only choice. You can help me decide the method, but I'll not go through what they went through. Deal?"

The last inch of the sun sank below the glittering water, the fading light washing the stones in somber amber shades. Ray rubbed his eyes, hoping to suddenly find better words to say, but none came. He reached for her hand. "I've never loved anyone like I love you, and I can't bear to lose you. I'll work as hard as I can while we fight this together." As he had hoped, inspiration struck. "Until then you have to swear to me to live the way we promised each other in our wedding vows, remember?"

A warm smile edged away her worried look. "You mean the part about never living a halfway life?"

He matched her smile. "Exactly. I'll dedicate my days to finding a cure and you dedicate yours to your music and your family … especially Madeline. Spend as much time with her as you can. We made those edits to her so she could get to know us if this disease took us early. We owe her and ourselves that, right?"

She held his hand tight as the first stars began to flicker in the darkening blue sky. "That's a deal I can live with."

CHAPTER TWELVE

Adam was the first to arrive at the offices of Silverstone Confidential, the high-end surveillance company the three had hired to learn more about their attackers. Ensley walked in a couple of minutes later, and he gave her a hug, extending the embrace just a little longer than usual. "It's good to see you, Ens. I've missed you." Her cheeks seemed brighter and he thought there was an extra sparkle in her nearly black eyes, or at least hoped so anyway. "How've you been?"

She ran a finger through her lustrous hair, pulling it behind her right ear. "Busy. We're trying to build a coalition against those WAGE activists. Sorry we had to push this off for a few weeks, but it seems they're getting stronger every day. The meeting I attended in Stockholm was just too important to miss."

"No worries. I was busy with a board meeting of my microbank where we met with Master Fong to discuss expansion in Asia."

Madeline walked into the room. "The gang's all here. Group hug!"

The three came together and Adam breathed in their intoxicating perfume scents, enjoying their embrace as another chance to hug Ens… until he felt a surprising, subtle tickle from Maddy. As they stepped away, his eyes darted between them, an unexpected swirl of emotions taking hold, his words almost tangled. "It's, it's really good to see you… both."

Clint Broyles entered the small conference room. "We're happy to have you as clients and are ready to prove why we're the best in the business. Shall we start the briefing?"

Clint looked to be about forty years old with just a couple of gray hairs at his temples. Adam noted the navy Italian cut suit over his muscular frame, reminding him of one of his own. He nodded. "I say it's past time."

They all sat down around the table where a thin, clear-cover binder awaited each of them. "This is a hard copy of what I'm about to show you. Let's begin." The lights dimmed as a slide with the image of two women appeared onscreen. It looked to be a photo taken at long range of Becky Brown and her wife walking hand-in-hand.

Clint used a laser pointer. "We took this picture of Becky Brown and Kelley Slaughter two weeks ago in Central Park. As you already know, they've been living here in the city for the past couple of years. You also know that they are the founders of WAGE."

Just hearing the word 'WAGE' caused all three to sit straighter, with Ens getting her feelings out first. "I hate those people. They've made our lives, and so many others so much tougher. It's no surprise they would be involved in this."

With the push of the button, Clint advanced the slide and two children in angel costumes appeared in a black and white photo. "What you may not know is these women have known each other almost their entire lives. This image was printed in a suburban Atlanta community newspaper twenty years ago. They were both in a Christmas show at their private school."

Maddy's anger seemed to be building. "Little angels can grow up to be raging thugs. Another reason I'm not all that hip on religion."

Clint's head tilted. "Evidently so. Seems they were both living comfortable upscale suburban Atlanta lives until their fathers were murdered on the same night. That's when things began to change drastically."

Ensley said what they had learned a month ago. "Maddy found

out they were murdered on the night Adam was born, right?"

"That's correct. Just over five years ago." Clint paused, then spoke in a more casual voice, compared to his all-business approach so far. "And just so you all know, I've followed your lives and find them fascinating. My wife and I are seriously looking at taking the leap of genetic editing with our next child. The possibilities are amazing."

They had all heard some version of this statement hundreds of times and Ensley gave the standard reply. "It's pretty amazing, but just know it's not always a garden of roses. Perfect genes don't equal perfect lives." She added a new twist. "And that's why we're here today."

"Right. Let's proceed." His business-first demeanor returned. "Following the deaths of their fathers their lives diverged, with Kelley openly embracing her life as a gay woman, while Becky spiraled downward in a fog of drugs and alcohol. After overdosing and nearly dying, it appears she and her childhood friend reconnected. That seemed to stabilize Becky's life, who soon came out as gay herself, and announced they were a couple. It was only a few months later when they founded WAGE."

Adam's thoughts turned back to the night that set everything in motion. "Any idea why their fathers were killed?"

"No, the killings were a mystery to the Atlanta police then, and remain so today. I looked at the evidence and the hits were clearly done by professionals. They were really good and left no trail. There were some theories about potential links to the mafia, but none were found, and no motive ever uncovered. I've seen a lot of operations, but few this clean."

"And did you find any connections to us?"

Clint answered quickly. "We did a lot of digging and haven't come up with anything. If these murders are somehow connected to you three, it's very well hidden."

Clint waited for a few beats, but no additional questions were asked. The next slide showed a collage of photos showing several other twenty and thirty somethings with Becky and Kelley in different locations. "Moving on, our surveillance has uncovered a core group of friends who we believe were also involved in the attack at Chalky's Wild World. There's an Anfernee Burrows and Phillip Poppins, to name a couple, all of which are included in your hard copy. While we feel strongly about this, we don't have absolute proof, which leads us to recommendations."

"Finally." While the backstory was interesting, what Adam wanted was action. "It's time we get some answers."

The next slide showed a white, non-descript commercial van. "On three of the past four Wednesday nights, Becky and Kelley walked to dinner at a restaurant a few blocks from their apartment. If that happens tomorrow night, we plan a snatch and grab on a stretch of sidewalk with no security camera coverage. We should have them sedated and heading to a location in New Jersey in less than twenty seconds."

The plan startled Adam. "You can do that?"

Clint's half smile and wink telegraphed his reply. "Legally? No. Would they ever press charges? Also no. We know what they did and blackmail is a powerful deterrent."

Maddy spoke first, smiling. "And we'll be waiting to have a little conversation."

Now Clint's smile went full. "The building is in an industrial area where you'll have plenty of privacy. We'll have them both strapped securely to chairs when they wake, so you'll be having the meeting on your terms. Our team will wait two blocks away, keeping an eye out for anything out of the ordinary. When you're finished, we'll help if there's any clean up."

Adam's eyes widened. "Clean up? Whoa. We just want to talk, that's all."

Clint's expression hardened, eyes narrowing. "In our experience, we've seen talks progress in unexpected directions. We want to assure you if anything unplanned were to happen, we'll be prepared to deal with it. Like I said, we are the best in the business."

The realization of what they were about to do weighed on Adam's shoulders as he addressed Clint. "You guys are the real deal." He nodded toward Ens and Maddy. "We haven't seen each other for a few weeks, mind if we hang here for a few minutes?"

"It's all yours." He pointed toward the reception area. "Just let Jenny know when you leave."

Clint closed the door as he left and Adam leaned back in his chair. "Snatch and grabs...clean up? I've never done anything like this."

"We saw you laying in a pool of blood, worried you might be dead." Ens glanced at Maddy. "I'm guessing Maddy is with me in saying these girls deserve what's coming."

Nodding, Maddy confirmed. "I don't want to stoop to their level of violence, but I want them to think we would. A little fear goes a long way."

Adam rubbed his head at the spot where Becky hit him, reminding himself of why they were doing this in the first place, his voice low and cold. "Then let's deliver enough fear that they get the message loud and clear."

CHAPTER THIRTEEN

Ansen had just finished a meeting with the Chief Accounting Officer of the bank when his phone buzzed in his pocket. He glanced at the caller ID and a sinking feeling hit, suspecting he was about to hear bad news. Hoping he was wrong, he answered with a rise in his voice. "Hi, Stephan. What's up?"

Kristoff Svoboda's youngest son replied in a tenor Ansen feared, words carrying awful news. "It's father... he's dead."

Ansen closed his eyes, picturing an image of the patriarch as the strong man he first met as a boy. "Oh Stephan, I'm so sorry for your loss."

There was a catch in Stephan's voice. "He's gone...I can't believe it."

He's barely holding it together. "How's your mother, the rest of the family?"

"Like me, stunned. We knew of his condition, but he told us he had years, that he was retiring soon to spend more time with us."

So that's what drove the recent retirement talk. "Your father was a great man and meant a lot to both Bree and myself. His loss will be felt around the world."

"Thank you." Stephan sniffled. "I called you first because I know how much you meant to him." A long sigh followed. "He felt tired today and decided to take a nap, and never awoke. This is a complete shock, and now I must call the other council members."

"I can help. I can share the load."

Stephan's voice was weary. "There is nothing that I would like more, but this is my responsibility... to my father, and to the council. Everyone needs to hear this directly from me."

"Bree and I will be there as soon as we can. Is there anything we can do to make this terrible moment any easier for you or the family?"

There was silence, then Stephan replied. "I can't think straight right now, but there will be plenty of decisions to be made in the coming days, and I'll seek your advice then."

"We'll be there for you and your family."

"See you soon."

Ansen hung up, his thoughts turning to the future. *The succession politicking will start immediately. I bet I have a dozen calls before the end of the day, one of them sure to be from Liza.*

Three hours later Bree and Ansen were on a private jet headed toward Kristoff's home outside of Prague. She smiled. "Remember the flight from China five years ago?"

"I recall how mad you were when you learned of our destination." Ansen laughed softly. "You thought he was trying to kill you."

Her eyes glistened. "We had just escaped a second assassination attempt and I was experiencing the strangest pregnancy ever. My emotions were all over the board." She pulled a tissue from her Prada handbag and dabbed the corners of her eyes. "I don't think anyone could have convinced me then I would come to love him like a second father. He did everything he said he would for Third Rock Sustainability, and more. He believed in what we are doing, and pushed the society toward real action to make the planet a better place."

Ansen held her hand. "He had a vision for the future and a kind heart, that's for sure, but he knew when he had to be tough. That balance is why he was so effective, and why he'll be so hard to replace. Leaders like him don't come around every day."

Bree hated politics in general, and didn't like the internal dynamics of the society any better. "Speaking of that, you've been on the phone almost non-stop. From the bits and pieces I've overheard, sounds like the race to be the next patriarch has already begun."

"It has. Some, like Liza, have been subtly laying the groundwork for years and are already in full campaign mode. Stephan must have contacted her second, because she called me less than ten minutes after I talked to him. She laid it on thick about how much Kristoff meant to her, and how much his leadership would be missed ... before suggesting that an experienced hand would be an asset for our next patriarch. I know what she's doing, and it turns my stomach."

The mention of Liza's name turned Bree's as well, recalling the night the older woman's plan nearly killed all three first babies and their parents. "Sometimes I still wake up in a cold sweat and swear I smell spent gunpowder. If the warning of her attack had come a few minutes later, we would all be dead, and those three special children never born. She can't win, can she?"

The tilt of his head told the story. "She's a skilled operator and has spent the past five years currying favor while reworking her reputation. She's got a chance."

Those words didn't comfort her, but other thoughts now bubbled to the surface. "Speaking of our special child, feels like something's up with him."

"What do you mean?"

"You know how much he likes Kristoff's estate, the same as we did when we were brought there by our parents."

Ansen smiled. "I still like it. If I need some stress relief during all the politicking, I may take one of the horses for a ride, or challenge you in skeet shooting." He laughed. "On second thought, maybe I'll shoot alone, I've never beaten you."

She gave a wink and a nod at his compliment. She had always been the better shot, but it never seemed to bother Ansen, just one more thing she loved about him. "There are lots of happy memories there, that's why I was surprised when he didn't push to join us in paying our respects... and maybe trying again to beat you on the shooting range." Her mind sensed something off, but she couldn't put a finger on it. "He said he had some other things going on."

"Well, it's probably for the best. As we were just discussing, there is very important society business to address, and we haven't had 'the talk' with him." He turned toward her, his words taking an air of resignation. "I know it's time to have that discussion, I'm just not sure if either he or *us* is ready."

They had been wrestling with that question for some time, and the recent attack only added more pressure, but lately a new idea had taken root. She decided to take advantage of this alone time. "I've been thinking, while it's just us, let me ask a delicate question. Does the world still need the Tree of Life Society?"

She felt his hand flinch, then his voice rose. "What? How can you say that? Just a few days ago our son was attacked because of his genome. Who else has the resources and determination to protect him, and all the others that have followed? We've never needed the society more."

The two of them rarely argued, but she felt it a legitimate question. "Hear me out. When you told me about the society you said it was formed to provide a better, longer life for the children. Right?"

He stared intently, answering quickly. "Yes, and people trying to kill them tells me we still need the society."

She took another stab at explaining. "Okay, think about it this way. Since Adam, the floodgates have opened with millions of other genetically modified children being born, almost all sure to have healthier and longer lives. I'm not minimizing the threat to Adam, or any other individual GM person, I'm just saying that the big picture is that we have fulfilled the founder's dream. Mission accomplished. We've changed the world."

His brow furrowed and jaw set. "Even if your argument has merit, and I'm not saying it does, now is not the time. There is a power struggle underway in the society, people are targeting our son, and governments are trying to make him a second-class citizen." His hard gaze softened. "Please, I'm begging, don't mention this while we're in Prague. I promise you it would only make things worse, and it's already going to be a Machiavellian war."

She nodded, knowing he was right. While never a cheerleader for the society, it had been a force for good in her life. It had given her a wonderful family, and with their help, a powerful voice in the environmental community that had resulted in real change. "Not a word, I swear. I'm here to support their family in this time of grief, and pay respects to a great man. We have plenty of time to think about these issues."

CHAPTER FOURTEEN

While Adam had his own apartment, having both parents out of the country made him feel even freer, like a teen sneaking out on a Saturday night for some fun. But this was a Wednesday night, and while he felt an adrenaline rush, tonight was all about business. He was dressed all in black, riding in the back of an SUV with dark tinted windows, between Ensley and Madeline dressed the same. His mind drifted back to the briefing on this plan and the feelings he felt when hugging each of them. *Maybe there can be some kind of party later if things go well tonight. The more I'm around them lately, the more I wonder about a special future with one of them.*

The driver spoke. "We're almost there." In a few more minutes he pushed a button on a remote control and the industrial garage door of a low-slung warehouse crawled open, allowing their entrance. "Follow me. We have everything arranged."

Maddy seemed in a fine mood as she addressed the similarly dressed Silverstone Confidential operative. "I love what you've done with the place." Adam and Ens snickered as she continued riffing. "Really, I think it's perfect"

What they saw was a darkened, wide-open empty space with a single bare bulb hanging from the ceiling over two hard plastic patio chairs. The guard seemed to recognize Maddy, and gave a shy smile. "Form and function, ma'am. We find it sets the right mood and makes clean up easy if things go sideways."

That possible option caught Adam off guard again. "Love the mood, but I doubt there will be any clean up."

The guard's phone pinged and he glanced at a text. "The packages are almost here. I'll be taking my position a couple blocks away. Just send a text when you're ready to leave." With that he got into the SUV and left.

A plain utility van pulled into the space a few seconds later and four operators moved swiftly to get the limp bodies of Becky Brown and Kelley Slaughter out of the back. Using duct tape, they strapped the women upright in the chairs, securely zip tying their arms and legs. They left their heads shrouded in loose hoods. The leader, known to them only as Alpha One used an alcohol prep and then gave each woman an injection. "They should be coming around soon."

Seeing the two women bound sent a shudder through Adam. He wanted revenge, but didn't anticipating feeling conflicted like this. *Maybe I haven't thought this through as much as I should.* He pushed the unbidden thought away. "We'll take it from here." With that the four men piled back into the van and drove away to wait, the metal garage door squeaking and clanking downward until it slammed shut.

The noise seemed to startle one of the tied-up women. Her words slurred. "What's happening... where am I?" Her head rose and turned side to side, the voice now alert and on edge, but muffled under the hood. "Kelley? Where are you Kelley!?"

Now the other hooded head rolled side to side. "Becky??? I can't see."

Maddy laughed. "Kind of sucks when something bad happens out of the blue, bitches!"

Ensley joined the action, getting right up in the covered face of Becky. "You should be thankful we're not using baseball bats and crowbars!"

Both seated figures sat still as statues until Becky snarled. "Take this hood off, if you're brave enough, pussies!"

Maddy danced around the chairs in a figure eight pattern and began belting the chorus to her latest hit, *Freak Flag.* "You see me, I see you. You see my freak flag flying, and I see yours too."

Becky's arms yanked, trying to free herself, not moving the binding a millimeter. Seeming to recognize her captor's voice, she raged as loud as a bullhorn. "You skanky bitch daughter of a no-talent whore. You're not even brave enough to face me."

The singing stopped as Maddy ripped off Becky's hood and slung it to the floor, the detained woman's eyes widened and nostrils flared. Maddy got up in her grill and yelled. "You can say anything you want about me, but when you say something about my mother, people get hurt!"

Becky's eyes blinked, adjusting to the bare light, then glared, her chin raising defiantly. "Give it all you got, you little cunt. I'm tougher than you'll ever be!"

Maddy took a quick step to her left and slapped the hooded Kelley so hard the chair tipped over, sending the captive tumbling to the floor, still completely bound. Sobbing erupted from under the hood, as Becky screamed. "Nooo!! Please stop! She's pregnant!"

Adam pulled the enraged Maddy away, wrapping her in both arms while Ens righted the toppled and crying Kelley. He whispered to Maddy. "Chill, girl. You know you and your mom have more talent in your pinkies than that pig will ever have." Thoughts from earlier returned. *Damn, I've always loved your fierceness.* He could feel her anger level drop, and out of the corner of his eye he saw bulging eyes of panic now gracing Becky's face. He spoke softly to Maddy. "You got her attention, that's for sure."

As he calmed Maddy, Ens stood over Becky, who continued straining to free herself. She slowly pounded her right fist into her left palm, creating a popping sound that echoed in the vast empty space, her words low and menacing. "I thought I broke your nose, glad to see I was right. Think of me every time you look in the mirror, bitch."

Becky's body tensed as she tried again to break her duct tape and nylon zip tie bonds, neither giving an inch. "I don't care what you do to me, but please leave her alone, for God's sake. Even freaks like you must have some morals."

Ensley spat on the angry woman. "Really? You want to talk morals? I'm sure you took the time to find out the pregnancy status of every girl you hurt on that barbaric run through Chalky's."

Ens walked away and a few seconds of silence passed as Adam's embrace of Maddy ended. He now took his turn standing in front of Becky, speaking as calmly as a monk. "Your actions have brought you here, and now your nasty attitude has resulted in someone you love getting hurt." He paced slowly in front of both women, removing Kelley's hood, seeing a trickle of blood from a busted lip, running down her chin. "What are we to do?"

Kelley whimpered. "Just let us go, please."

He stopped, standing again in front of Becky with arms crossed, enjoying the interrogation more than he knew he should. "Let me ask you something, Mrs. Brown. A month ago, you bashed my head with a crowbar. If the tables were turned and I was tied up here, what would you do? Would you finish the deed by swinging over and over again until my brains spilled onto the floor? Would that make you happy?"

Becky shook her head and laughed dismissively. "I would love nothing more than to do that, but you and I both know that if I did, I would be signing my own death warrant. With a baby on the way, I wouldn't risk mine and Kelley's future, even for that pleasure."

His eyebrow arched as this was not the answer he expected. He began pacing in front of them again, pondering her words. *Death warrant? What the hell is she talking about? Play it cool and see what else we can find out.* He stopped in front of Becky again. "And who, exactly, would be executing this death warrant?"

A thick blue vein arose on her forehead, descending from her silver-gray scalp to the gap between her eyebrows as she continued to strain against her bindings. "Your parents, of course, as soon as they figured out who did it... and I'm sure they would. Who do you think I'm talking about?" The surprising answer must have registered on Adam's face, because now Becky leaned back in her plastic chair, seeming to relax. "You freaks don't know, do you?"

Adam regained his outward composure, but knew he had lost the advantage in this conversation. He paced again, giving himself time. *My parents? Mr. and Mrs. Prim and Proper? I've got to figure this out, fast. THINK!* Then he remembered the fact that Maddy had discovered and decided to try to bluff his way forward. *Here goes nothing.* He bent down, his face inches from hers, delivering his line as cool and clear as mountain spring water. "You mean like when they killed both your fathers?"

He slowly stood upright, eyes locked on hers, seeing her previous confidence appearing to wane. Her chin lowered as she answered flatly, the haughtiness of moments before gone. "Yeah, exactly like that."

Hell yes! It worked! ... but there's too much I don't know. Time to take the win, keep the advantage and figure out the rest of this away from them. "Hey guys." He looked towards Ens and Maddy. "What's some of the other names on the list? You know some of the known associates of these two knuckle-heads?"

Maddy rattled off a name in a derisive tone. "Off the top of my head there's some punk named Anfernee." She snapped her fingers, as she looked at Ens. "What's another one?"

"Yeah, let me think." Ensley thought for a second. "Oh, a Phillip Poppins comes to mind. We can check the complete list later."

Adam turned back to Becky and seeing her eyes downcast he knew he had her where he wanted. "This has just been a demonstration, one given in good faith." He now spoke directly to Kelley, wanting to drive home how much was at stake. "Congratulations on the baby, it's a joyful thing. I understand the first trimester can be very dangerous."

She avoided his gaze as he let the moment hang. Slowly, he knelt down in front of both of them, speaking like a judge giving prisoners a warning with their reprieve. "We know a lot about the two of you. We know who you are and what you've done. We know the friends who help you do your dirty work, and we now know you have something very special to live for." He looked at Becky. "Let's see how smart you are, Becky Brown. What do you know about us?"

Her words came thick and slow. "We know that if we come at you again..." She paused, swallowed hard, then started again. "We know that if we come at you again, you'll kill us, and our friends."

Adam stood and clapped once. "There. Now that wasn't so hard, was it?" He glanced at Ens and Maddy for dramatic effect. "I told you we were dealing with reasonable people, that there would be no blood to clean up." He turned back to the two captives, speaking with a bounce. "I'm glad we had this little talk." Now he pointed to the bound pair, recalling the conversation back at Silverstone Confidential. *A little fear goes a long way.* His voice lowered to a growl. "And if we have to talk again, we're spreading sheets of plastic, because there will be so much blood this place will look like the set of a slasher movie."

CHAPTER FIFTEEN

Kristoff's gold inlaid oak casket was lowered into the ground of the Svoboda family cemetery. Johana Svoboda, his wife of fifty-one years, stood with their three children as a three-volley rifle salute echoed through the peaceful valley of the massive estate. No expense had been spared and no ritual overlooked as the Patriarch of The Tree of Life was laid to eternal rest.

Ansen glanced to his left, then right, taking in the rare site of all of the council members gathered in a single location. *Now the battle begins. The king is dead, long live the king... or queen. The only question is who it will be.* With the priest's final 'amen' the assembled members began milling around under a warm sun. A line of mourners in black suits and dresses formed with men and women giving the family solemn final condolences for their loss.

As soon as Ansen and Bree paid their respects, Liza and her husband, Rolf, approached them. "He was a great man, wasn't he?"

I trust her about as far as I can throw her. "Yes, he was. Like a second father to both Bree and myself."

Bree added her thoughts. "Without him, neither myself, Ansen, or our son would be alive. Some deeds will never be forgotten."

Touché. Ansen loved the not-so-veiled reference to the attack that Liza had ordered against them the night Adam was born, and he also enjoyed seeing Liza squirm.

"Yes... he had the ability to see the best in all of us, even in our worst moment, and for that I am eternally grateful." Appearing undeterred, Liza continued. "And now we begin the task of continuing our work without that steady hand. Ansen, perhaps we can discuss this further over a drink, later?"

Ansen was as diplomatic as ever, still uncertain who he would consider supporting. "Of course. I'm sure there will be many conversations before the vote."

Her eyes darted over his shoulder. "Yes. Now if you'll excuse me, I have a question I need to ask Charlotte."

Without waiting for his reply, she fluttered away. Bree held Ansen's hand as they walked back toward the mansion. "She sure is ballsy, I'll give her that. I see why you think she has a shot at succeeding Kristoff."

"In the old reformed group, she ousted Ben Brown, then had the political savvy to bring him back onboard, reporting to her. She survived the bloodshed of reunion, then used her strategic position to end up on this board. I'll never underestimate her after all she's done."

They took their time walking past the skeet shooting area where they both had so many happy memories. Bree stopped, looking downrange. "Pardon the pun, but who else is gunning for the position?"

A soft laugh showed her he appreciated the humor. "That's a pretty apt description of what's likely to happen. Imka has already asked me to support her candidacy, and she'll probably wrangle a fair share of the old guard. While I don't think Stephan has a chance, he may mount a run, hoping for a sympathy vote with the loss of his father. A couple of others may throw their hats into the ring if a clear leader fails to emerge quickly. Each has their flaws, so I'll wait and see how the next two days play out before I decide who to back. It's a tough job and I don't envy whoever sits in the chair next."

"One more reason I'll never be on the council. The palace intrigue would drive me crazy, and even worse, I would probably fire my mouth off and get us excommunicated. I'll stick to something easier, like saving the planet." In the distance they saw a figure marching toward them, causing Bree to frown. "Speaking of worse. Here comes the Dragon Lady."

Her small feathered hat with black netting over her face gave the blunt woman, who almost always wore black anyway, an even more imposing air. She skipped all small talk and got right to her point. "We need to talk about who will be the next patriarch."

Ansen put his hands up in mock surrender. "Slow down. I've not decided who to support, in fact I'm not even sure who will stand."

She looked around as if searching for eavesdroppers, then lowered her voice. "You miss my point. I'll not break my vows, but I'll tell you something, then see if you are smart enough to ask the right questions."

Just when I thought she couldn't get crazier. "Okaaaay. I'll play along. What *can* you tell me?"

"As a council member you know most of the secrets and inner workings of the society." She stopped and looked at him with eyes open wide and head cocked.

He returned her stare, then he got it. "Oh, now is when we find out if I'm smart enough to ask the right questions." He shot a quick glance at Bree and gave a sharp raise of the eyebrows signaling he had no idea what was going on. "Let me think. Okay, that means there are things that even council members don't know, right?"

She nodded and answered with a single word. "Correct." Then she stood still, her face a mask, looking at him.

"Now I get it, you'll only answer my exact question." He grinned, thinking he could unlock the secret with one question. "What do you want me to know?"

The doctor sighed, seeming disappointed. "I've sworn a vow. It's something I can only tell the next patriarch. You'll have to do better than that."

Her look told him it was his turn again in the game. Bree tugged at him, then whispered in his ear. Ansen listened and agreed, now asking their next question. "Does the secret have to do with our family?"

"Yes."

The two again looked at each other for a second, then Ansen asked another question. "When the next patriarch learns this secret will they tell me?"

"Probably not."

The charade continued. "Do you feel it is important that we know?"

"Absolutely."

"I see." Again, Ansen looked at Bree, now with seriousness, realizing this was not some trivial wordplay. Suddenly his eyes widened, understanding what she was trying to tell him. "Thank you for answering a few questions, Dr. Chavez, and I appreciate you not breaking your vow. Now, if you'll excuse us, I need to get back to the others and begin my campaign to be the next patriarch."

Bree clutched his arm in an iron grip and he was unsure if it was to keep herself from falling over, or physically trying to pull him back from his decision.

The crooked smile they knew so well returned. "Once again, I see that you two are smart enough to make the right decisions for yourselves, and for the good of the society."

CHAPTER SIXTEEN

The hoods were slipped off of Becky and Kelley's heads in a dark alley six blocks from their Hell's Kitchen apartment. Becky felt the ties binding her hands behind her back being snipped, then heard the only words from the armed men during the entire ordeal. "If you know what's good for you, you'll walk away and not look back."

She glanced at Kelley and nodded, then sneered without looking at her captors. "Thanks for a lovely evening, but let's never do it again."

Becky grabbed Kelley's hand and they walked fast toward the next well-lit block, saying nothing until turning onto the busy street. Her mind replayed the events of the night in such frighteningly graphic detail, she broke out in a sweat. When feeling safe, urgent words poured out. "God, all that matters is that you're okay. I couldn't bear for anything bad happening to you."

Kelley had held it together, but now that she was free, tears began to fall. "I can't do this again."

Becky's arm went around her wife, pulling her as close as possible while walking at a rapid clip. "We're almost home. Hang on just a little longer."

"I'll try." Kelley wiped her eyes with the back of her hand and sniffled. "That was the scariest thing ever."

They reached their building and in short order were slamming their door tight, locking it securely. Sitting on the sofa in a mutual embrace with Coco straddling their laps, Becky stroked Kelley's soft auburn hair. "We're safe now, just let it all out."

That seemed to be all the encouragement Kelley needed as sobs now wracked her body, tears flowing in twin torrents down her pale cheeks. "I... I thought they were going to kill us."

While Kelley seemed immobilized in fear, Becky's mood had already transitioned to anger. "I can't believe the nerve of those freaks. Who do they think they're messing with!"

Kelley's whole body shook as Becky's outburst only heightened her response. "Please, please! They'll kill us... they'll kill our friends." She clutched Becky tighter. "Tell me we'll be alright, that our baby will be okay."

This stress can't be good for our child, not at all. I need to calm down and tell her what she wants to hear. Becky's voice now sounded tranquil and smooth, as if cloaked in comforting velvet. "Our child is the most important thing in the world. I won't do anything to put you or the baby in danger."

The tremors abated and Kelley's grip loosened a little, her bloodshot eyes blinking glossy tears as she looked up at Becky. "You're my rock and I'm going to need you more than ever these next few months. Promise me you'll stay away from all of them. It's too dangerous."

Becky continued slowly running her hand over her wife's hair. "Don't worry about them. We've got too much on the line to risk getting you hurt. I promise." Becky's eyes stared unfocused as if into an uncertain future. *I'll promise her anything she wants, but we'll see how things look tomorrow. My father taught me many valuable lessons, and one of the most important is there must always be payback.*

CHAPTER SEVENTEEN

The mood in the SUV was unsettled as the three of them rode back to the city. On the one hand, they had achieved exactly what they set out to do; show Becky and Kelley that there are consequences, and there would be more in the future, if they tried to harm the three of them again. They had also learned that Kelley was expecting, giving them even more leverage. On the other hand, there was the unexpected discovery that their boring, upstanding parents may have had something to do with the assassinations of Becky and Kelley's fathers. That didn't make sense at all, so Adam proposed their next stop. "How about a nightcap at Chalky's? We have a lot to talk about."

Ensley rubbed the back of her neck. "Yeah. Everything was going as planned until that part about our folks. I don't know what to make of that."

"Same." Maddy was looking out the window, her mind seeming to be somewhere else. "I'm going to pass on Chalky's tonight."

Adam turned toward her and spoke sympathetically. "What's up Maddy? You seem upset."

"No, I'm not upset." She bit her bottom lip. "It's my mom. I'm worried about her. When I saw her last week, I found out she was experiencing early symptoms of Huntington's."

Adam's and Ensley's words of sympathy jumbled together. "So sorry... no... can't be."

"Hearing the bitch say nasty things about her tonight made me want to see her again. I'm going to head to the airport and catch the redeye so I can be there in the morning. I just need to see her."

So that's why she belted Kelley so hard. Adam offered support. "That's awful news. Is there anything we can do, anything you need?"

Ens offered more of the same. "You know we've got your back. Please let us help."

Maddy shook her lowered head. "This was their worst fear... why they went the genetic modification route with me. Other than praying for a miracle, I don't think anyone can help."

Adam sighed. "This sucks, big time." Then a thought occurred. "Look, the last thing your mom needs now is questions about Becky and Kelley's fathers. Leave that to us and you just spend as much quality time with your folks as you can."

Ensley reached over Adam for her friend's hand. "Want us to take you straight to the airport, or to your apartment?"

"I'm cutting it short, so straight to the airport would be great." Sounding as if she were about to cry, Maddy added, "we've had some clashes every now and then, but things have never been better between me and mom. This is all just tearing me up inside."

They redirected the driver, then rode in near silence until pulling into the 'departing passenger' lane at Newark. They all rolled out of the car and hugged, wishing Maddy the best as she flew to Los Angeles to reunite with her mother. Ens summed it up. "Cherish every moment with her."

"Thanks, guys. You're the best." With that Maddy rushed inside as Adam and Ens climbed back into the SUV.

He looked over at her. "Chalky's?"

Her eyes said yes, but her words disagreed. "I would love that, but I'm on a dawn flight to Tokyo. It's a big GM anti-discrimination conference, and I haven't even started packing. Those WAGE people have momentum and I need to be there. I feel I was born for this fight."

He thought about trying to talk her into changing her mind, then decided against it, stating a hard, cold fact. "I understand. These are the lives we've chosen."

She reached for his hand and held it as they drove. "But I would like a rain check when I get back."

His grin was automatic. "I would like that very much." They rode back toward the city, holding hands the entire way and it was all he could do to not lean over and kiss her, but he checked that urge. *We're too good of friends to blow this... and maybe she thinks this is all it should ever be. I wish I could read her mind.*

As they got closer to her place, he made the same basic argument about learning more about their parent's role in those assassinations. "Look, you're going to be super busy for the next few days, so how about I take the lead with the folks on those killings. I'll see my parents first, and the shootings did happen on the day I was born."

She leaned over and kissed him on the cheek. "Sounds like a plan. You can give me the scoop when I get back."

He and the driver waited until she stepped safely into her building. The driver spoke. "Where to, sir?"

While the full adrenaline rush from earlier had subsided, he was nowhere near tired, or wanting to be alone. "Too early to go home to an empty apartment on a night like tonight. Take me to Chalky's."

They pulled up and Adam prepared to roll right on in, then a chill ran up his spine, remembering the attack that happened here. "There's an extra thousand in it if you'll watch my back for a couple of hours."

The reply was automatic. "It would be my pleasure, sir."

They walked in and the place had a good crowd for a Wednesday night, but not thumping like on the weekends. Kiss Me Kimee saw Adam and made a bee-line. "The VIP section is always open for you, Mr. Clayborn. Right this way."

Following her as she swished her mini-skirt covered hips to the beat, Adam decided he liked the view. *I'm single and while there might be something starting with Ensley, it's anything but certain.* "Please, just call me Adam."

She turned, her face looking flushed. "I'll let Chalky know you're here, and Yori is hanging somewhere." They reached a prime table and Adam took a seat. She leaned in close, whispering through her neon green painted lips. "I'm off the clock in twenty, if you would like me to join the party."

Pleased, his cheeks dimpled. "I would like that *very* much."

The kiss was immediate, and her tongue searched aggressively. She stood, giving a carefree giggle. "You know what they say, every night's a party at Chalky's."

CHAPTER EIGHTEEN

Ansen entered a familiar space to begin the process to choose the next patriarch. *This is the same room where we held Bree's initiation ceremony.* Back then it felt warm and cozy, but with the furniture and lighting changed, it now felt cold and stark. *A very appropriate vibe for the cut-throat tactics I may see today.*

As the senior member of the council, Imka spoke first. Standing, her red suit looked especially vibrant against her dark skin, which combined with the graying of her hair presented an image of both power and experience. "We are gathered here for one of the most important responsibilities of this august body. As our assembly has done on twenty-four prior occasions, we will select our twenty-fifth patriarch, and I will serve as moderator for this conclave."

Imka set the order of events. "Those wishing to be considered as candidates will self-nominate, and by random draw, be given up to five minutes to state their case." She glanced at Ansen, Stephan and Liza, the three others who had already made their intentions known. "After opening statements, the candidates will field questions. We will then adjourn, allowing for individual consultations."

After a pause, Imka continued. "Tomorrow, we will have final statements, then an open vote." Her expression brightened with a broad smile. "With our task completed, we'll join for the coronation, followed by a celebration ball. We shall head home the next morning, united in our determination to lead our order into the future."

Ansen scanned the other faces around the table, seeing some

serene, others with furrowed brows, and several nodding to her words. *I have to win, and the table is set with knives at the ready. Let the games begin.*

Liza spoke up. "We're here because of the loss of one of the greatest patriarchs ever. I respectfully submit my name for consideration, understanding the challenge of living up to his example."

Stephan spoke next. "No one feels my father's loss more than I, and no one has benefited more from his wisdom. That makes me uniquely qualified to follow in his footsteps."

As expected, Stephan. Guess it's my turn. Thinking ahead to this moment, Ansen had anticipated being nervous, but instead felt surprisingly calm, despite the high stakes of which Dr. Chavez hinted. "Our society has had one goal for the entirety of its existence, to achieve a better life for our children. I submit that no one on this board has done more to advance that goal than I, and none are in as strong of a position to continue that role."

Rising, Imka declared herself the final candidate. "It is my duty to place my name into consideration. I have witnessed the successes and failures of our order, and that lengthy history provides me with perspective that no one else can match."

No others spoke, closing the nomination session. Imka held a black velvet bag with the Tree of Life insignia stitched in red. She picked up four smooth stones from the table. "Each candidate will reach in and draw one of these numbered tokens, determining the order of opening statements. As the interim leader, I draw last." Her eyes circled the table. "If there are no questions, I ask Liza to come forward.

Reaching the front, Liza put her hand in pulling out a smooth rock, then held it up. "I've drawn number four."

Ansen tried to mask his disappointment. *Damn. Speaking last is always an advantage, and I need every edge I can get.*

Stephan stepped forward. "I've drawn number one."

A subtle nod signaled Ansen's approval. *Everyone will have forgotten most of what he says by the time we finish.*

Now it was his turn. Standing alongside the others, he reached in, hoping luck was with him. Holding his marker aloft, he smiled. "I go third." He released a relieved sigh. *If this becomes a choice between Liza and myself, it's best if we make our cases one after the other.*

Imka pulled the last rock from the bag, revealing her number two position. "With the order selected, we will begin. Stephan, you have up to five minutes to state your case."

Stephan began with a tremble in his voice. "Kristoff Svoboda was a great leader and father, and the continuation of his vision will carry the Tree of Life Society forward into a successful future."

That's all he's got. Point number one, two and three will be about continuity. I like him, but if he weren't Kristoff's son, he wouldn't even be on this council. Ansen listened as Stephan rephrased his premise three different ways, as expected.

Imka went next. "I've had a say in every decision made by this council for many years, starting with how we handled the split with the reformed movement." She looked directly at Liza. "I've also been a vocal leader on the continuous funding of Dr. Chavez that culminated in the births of this wonderful new generation of children."

She's going with the 'seasoned hand' approach. Of course, she'll leave out the part about her temper. We'll see how she does when questions get harder. Her pitch went the full five minutes, chocked full of examples of tough votes. He listened, leaving him with a final thought. *A valuable voice, but flying off the handle is not what we need.*

Now it was his turn, and once again his expected nerves failed to materialize. "Good morning fellow council members. The vote that you cast for the next patriarch will be like none in our history." He looked at Zadie and pointed. "It's all because of her child, and mine, and the other member children like them that have been born in the last five years, and the technology we unleashed is changing the very course of humanity. The challenges we will face in the coming years will be nothing like those we've encountered in the past."

Ansen's hand went to his heart. "You all know what happened two weeks ago. Adam, Ensley and hundreds of other young people were attacked." He now took a clear shot at Liza. "In fact, their lives have been in danger since they were conceived, and I've been at the front lines of defending them from the beginning, barley escaping murder myself."

His hand now went to his side as he glanced over at Stephan. "There is nothing inherently wrong with continuity, in fact it's usually a good thing. But let's be clear, the challenges we will face are different than those of the past. Moving forward, our biggest worries will be how we confront the discrimination against these special children, and continuity offers only outdated ideas."

Ansen surveyed the room and saw all eyes aimed at Stephan. *Sorry, I have to win to find out what Chavez knows.* He turned toward Imka. "What our society needs is someone with a steady hand, someone with vast connections throughout the world, someone who seeks to understand the landscape before lashing out, and someone who is intimately connected to today's new reality. I submit that due to my extensive business connections, being the father of our first special child, and documented history of fighting for all of these exceptional children, I am uniquely qualified to lead our society. I humbly ask for your support."

It was Liza's turn, and she stared at Ansen. "While much has been said about the changes our new children have brought to the society, I remind everyone of the other significant transformation that's happened. The schism that caused years of strife and violence against our own has been mended. Once again, we operate as a unified society."

She now turned her gaze toward Stephan. "Kristoff and I did the hard work of reconciling members who sometimes hated each other. Over ninety percent of reformed members have returned to the fold, and without my leadership that would never have happened. Can you imagine where we would be if we were still waging civil war?"

Standing ramrod straight, Liza's green suit with gold piping on the shoulder gave her the look of a field general. She turned to an angle Ansen expected. "Leadership is sometimes lonely and requires one to make the hardest of decisions, even sending our own into dangerous situations for the greater good. A life spent making those choices prepares me like no one else."

As expected, now she'll wrap up and we'll start the questioning.

But that didn't happen. Instead, Liza looked at Imka and then Sameer, softening her voice. "While the day will surely come for the next generation to lead, those of us who have lived through good times and bad know how fire hardens steel. I'm asking that when you make your choice, you'll consider not just my track record and history, but also the person I am now."

Whoa. Making a play for Sameer's vote is one thing, but by courting Imka she's thinking the same as me. It's between her and me.

Imka stood. "All four candidates have addressed the council, so we shall turn to questions. As I am also a candidate, Sameer will moderate this session."

Sameer nodded. "I'll start the questions with one for you. Imka, do you recall your proposal when Master Li was assassinated by a hit squad from the reformed movement?"

Her eyes glared. "Of course, I do." She shot a hard look toward Liza. "Master Li was beloved by both sides of the society. Those terrorist reformers had crossed a line, so I advocated we take out one of their board members." Her nostrils flared and breathing increased, as if she were reliving the incident. "And I would make the same recommendation today." In just a few seconds, she demonstrated her passion...and instinctive rush to violence.

Right to the heart of the matter; her fiery temperament.

With the template set, the questions that peppered each candidate went to the central concerns of each. Zadie's question, was an example of those fired at Liza, laying bare her checkered past. "Liza, at one time we were close and I considered you a mentor. Would you please tell this council who cast the tie-breaking vote on the final attempt to kill Gwen Blaze, Bree Battle, myself and our children, not to mention our spouses?"

Liza spun the question around with an answer about her experience making tough questions, never saying aloud that she was the one who cast that vote.

Charlotte aimed a pointed question to Ansen. "Other than provide the sperm for the first special child, and adroitly climbing the international banking ladder with society help, what have you done to demonstrate you are the right choice to lead us?"

"Just to refresh everyone's memory, I didn't find out I was Adam's father until Bree was in labor. What did I do before I knew that important fact? I was the one who introduced Bree to the society, and then played a key role in her joining of her own free will. We would be in a completely different place had that not happened."

He shot a glance to Liza. "Then, I was by Bree's side in the Nevis shootout and played a key role in her escape from the attack that killed Master Li, both of which were ordered by the reformers."

He turned to Zadie. "And I played a key role in bringing both Zadie and Gwen Blaze under our protection, eventually being part of the team that saved their lives, and the lives of those special babies in the Caribbean attack. In fact, I brought down the last attacker that bloody night."

Turning back to Charlotte, Ansen continued. "After finding out that I was Adam's father, I have raised him to the best of my ability. He's maturing into a fine young man who's been a great ambassador for the cause. Who here, other than me, can continue aiding in his development as a beacon to other society families to take this course?"

Ansen looked around the table. "And who here *hasn't* had their career helped by the society? We've all benefited our entire life, just as our forefathers hoped, and it would be more of a surprise if I hadn't been successful." His hands clasped in front. "I believe that I've proven my dedication and bravery, and it's clear I'm uniquely positioned to lead us as we confront our brave new future." Most other questions followed the same general themes, with few directed at Stephan. *I guess he's the obvious fourth place finisher.*

When the questioning ended, Sameer handed control back to Imka. "We are fortunate to have four strong, qualified individuals stepping forward seeking to lead our illustrious society. The rest of the day will be devoted to individual consultations with voting tomorrow. If there is no additional business, we will adjourn."

Stephan stood. "May I address the group?"

Imka nodded.

"My father's death was a shock, but none were impacted more than me. I felt it my duty to offer my name based on the belief that continuity would be useful in guiding our society." He glanced toward Ansen, his head bobbing subtly. "But hearing the other candidate's views, I am convinced that another aspirant is better positioned for the role. Therefore, I am withdrawing my name from consideration."

I didn't see that coming.

Imka accepted the withdrawal. "Your request is granted." She paused, seeming to give time for any other surprise announcements. "We move forward with three worthy candidates. With no other business…we are adjourned."

Let the consultations, horse trading and bribery commence.

On cue, Liza raced to Stephan's side.

CHAPTER NINETEEN

Morning rays of sunlight fought through the nearly closed wooden slats of the blinds in Adam's bedroom. His internal clock always seemed to wake him early, even after a night of partying, like last night. What was different this morning was the silhouette of Kiss Me Kimee under the sheets on the other side of the bed. *It wasn't just a pleasant dream.*

He watched the slow rise and fall of her curvy shrouded body as she breathed, replaying in his mind the caresses of her milky skin and nibbles on her earlobes. His thoughts wondered to a list he kept in the back of his mind. *Spur of the moment hook-ups. Another thing I can check off of things I missed in my warp speed youth.*

Rolling out of bed as quietly as possible, he headed for the shower. *No reason both of us have to be up at the crack of dawn.* After a long shower and quick shave, he exited the bathroom, surprised to see his companion for the night already dressed, except for her high-heels. "Sorry I woke you."

"You didn't wake me, I set my phone alarm." Kimee reached down and strapped her glittery shoes. "I've got class this morning and I think it would be a good idea if I changed." She stood, then did a pirouette beside the bed. "I'll let myself out."

"Wait! At least let me get you a coffee or something."

She glanced at her phone screen. "I guess I have time for an espresso and a bagel." She seemed to catch a glimpse of herself in the mirror. "Maybe I'll make it a double shot."

Adam grabbed his keys from the dresser. "I know a great shop right around the corner."

In just a few minutes they were seated at a café table spreading cream cheese over whole grain bagels. Kimee had downed her espresso and now took a sip of bottled spring water. "Thanks for the breakfast, but you didn't have to. I would have understood."

This wasn't Adam's first sexual encounter, but he was still new to next morning etiquette, especially in a situation like this where things happened spontaneously, with absolutely no thought of what's next. "No worries, I was hungry too." *This is awkward, so change the subject.* "What are you studying?"

Picking at the round snack, she looked down. "I want to be a psychologist, but right now core classes at community college are all I can afford."

We're from completely different worlds. "I bet you'll be good at it. You seem to have a way with people." *That came out all wrong.*

As her eyes rose to meet his, her small laugh confirmed she caught his gaff. "Look, we had some fun last night, but I know that's all it was. It's sweet that you want to share breakfast this morning, but you're on TV all the time and hang out with stars like Maddy Blaze. I work as a hostess at a freak bar. Last night our paths aligned for a few hours, but today we go back to our own orbits."

He knew she was right, but at the same time he truly felt they had *some* things in common. "We're both freaks, you know. We share that."

She gave him a side-eye. "I'll agree that we're both freaks, but let's also agree that like autism, there's a spectrum, and we're on totally different ends. I can't get a used car loan, and you run that bank thing. We barely live on the same planet."

Again, he knew she was right. Thanks to his parents, he was born into wealth with an instant network around the globe, but he still felt a connection. Finally, the lightbulb lit. "When I go out in public, people stare at me, already having an opinion. Some think I'm great. They think being genetically modified means I don't have problems, that everything is perfect and they want that for themselves. Others, like those that attacked us a few weeks ago, would like nothing better than to rid the world of me, and all GM people. They think we're some kind of invasive species, and it's best to exterminate all of us before we destroy humanity." His eyes met hers, seeing what he interpreted as a flicker of understanding. "I love the way you dress and do crazy things with your hair, you stand out. But I'm guessing you get some stares as well."

Her sharpened purple fingernails picked at the label on the water bottle. "Yeah, every day. I guess we're both just products of our genetics and the randomness of the universe. But we are who we are, and we get to choose how we live, no matter where we start life's journey."

"I feel the same way. I'll be the one to decide how I live."

Kimee glanced at her phone. "Hey, thanks for breakfast, but I really have to get moving."

As she wrapped up the remains of her bagel, he pulled out his phone and clicked the Uber app. "Just plug-in your address and call a car. I don't want my future psychologist to be late to class."

Her smile was sweet. "Last night was fun, but I liked this morning even better. Maybe I had a few preconceived ideas about you, but after getting to know you a little better, I think maybe I was wrong about a few things." The phone alert sounded, indicating the car had arrived, so she stood, preparing to leave. "I suppose we have more in common than I thought."

He stood as well, just like his mother taught him to do in the presence of a lady. "I'm glad to have a new friend. I'll see you at Chalky's."

She walked away, and like last night her miniskirt swished to each step, but today his mind was in a totally different place. Their discussion had triggered other thoughts, like all of the breaks he had gotten, and the talk with Becky Brown about his parents. *I need to get some answers, because I'm sensing the universe isn't as random as I imagine.*

CHAPTER TWENTY

Every council member, besides those still in the running for patriarch, had talked with Ansen before dinner. More questions came as drinks loosened tongues afterwards. Now, as the new day began, he felt no closer to knowing how they would vote, and that had him on edge.

Imka stood, calling the group to order. "It's an exciting day for our society. Today, we will perform our most sacred duty in electing our next patriarch, who will lead our group into a glorious future. A future filled with children who will make this planet a better place, fulfilling the vision of our founders, and all succeeding generations through the centuries."

The elegant woman paused and gave a lingering look to every member that Ansen interpreted as serene. *What is she up to now?*

"After an afternoon of consultations and an evening of mingling with our spouses, I have come to the conclusion that someone other than myself should take the reins as leader."

Ansen's stomach dropped as it dawned on him what this could mean. *The older vote might now coalesce behind Liza, making this a very close race. That's not the way I wanted to start this day.*

After dropping this bombshell at the last minute, Imka's tranquil visage seemed out of place to him. Her words belying no hint of her motives. "That now leaves two capable candidates that will present closing statements prior to our open vote. In accordance with tradition, the two remaining aspirants will speak in reverse order from yesterday, which means that Liza will address us first." She gestured. "Liza, the floor is yours."

As Liza made her way to the head of the table, Ansen's mind spun a dark possibility. *Has a deal been made between these two? This isn't good at all.*

In her black suit and white blouse, Liza was the picture of seasoned experience. "I am honored to stand before you as a candidate at this vitally important time in history. Our founders were men and women with a vision for their children, all children, growing up to live long and prosperous lives. Through the hundreds of years of our order's existence we've made progress in achieving that goal, in large part because of the steady hand of each prior patriarch. Leaders like the great Albert Brahms, who ascended to leadership at age fifty-five, leading us through the first years of the enlightenment, a time of great progress for the world and our families. Leaders like Daiyu Huang, assuming the role at sixty-two, who demonstrated the progressive nature of the society as both the first female and first Asian matriarch, over one hundred years before American women even had the right to vote. I aspire to live up to the standards that these, and all others who have taken the mantle of leadership, have set."

All about experience and age. No surprise. He gulped as he glanced at the older council members who were nodding to her words. *And it seems to be working.*

"With my long and varied history of leadership through challenging times, I stand before you as the candidate most prepared to lead the Tree of Life Society in these dangerous times." Liza gave a small bow of the head, then walked back to her seat.

Thinking of the stakes, he could feel his heart beating. *I wish I knew what was going on with Imka.*

Standing again, Imka's appearance gave nothing away. "It's time to hear from our final remaining candidate. Ansen, the floor is yours."

He made the short walk to the head of the table, buttoning his charcoal gray suit jacket, and making eye contact with each of the voters. Smiling, he became aware that yesterday's calm had abandoned him as he started nervously, speaking just a bit too fast. "I am also honored to stand before you as a candidate to succeed the great Kristoff Svoboda. As you all know, that great man became our leader at the relatively young age of forty-two, and I'm sure he faced some of the same questions that you might have about me."

No dancing around the issue, just meet the objection head on...and slow down for God's sake. He took a calming breath, then continued. "With the benefit of hindsight, we all now recognize him as one of the greatest ever to serve as patriarch. The council members he addressed in a forum exactly like this didn't have that luxury, but they obviously saw something in him that led them to believe he was the right person for their era, and we are the beneficiaries of that decision. He was tough, smart, and at the same time compassionate, as each situation demanded. That's the kind of leadership that I admire."

Okay, I'm feeling better. Time to go for broke. His eyes locked on Liza. "We all witnessed that in the aftermath of the Caribbean attack. He made the call to end Benjamin Brown and Ezra Slaughter's lives, then was smart enough to know there was a chance to mend the split in the society if he made the right moves. He showed compassion by sparing Liza's life, even though she cast the decisive vote on the attack in the first place, knowing it would be key to the greater good for us all."

Glancing at his audience, he saw nearly equal parts smiles and frowns. *Wrap it up and see how it goes, I get the feeling everyone has made up their minds.* "The Tree of Life Society has launched the world into a new era, and it's time for a new kind of leader. One who has a personal stake in seeing this special generation not just succeed, but thrive. I submit to you that as Kristoff Svoboda was the right leader for his time, I'm the right choice for this brave new world."

Imka set the stage for selection of their next leader. "The process for choosing our next patriarch was established centuries ago. It provides us the opportunity to hear their words, question them on any subject and consult with them individually. We've completed those stages and now it's time to cast our votes in this open forum. Sameer, we begin with you. For whom do you vote?"

The older man with the easy laugh leaned his elbow on the arm of the leather conference chair. "Due to her experience, I cast my vote for Liza."

Damn it!

Imka nodded, then turned her gaze to Sameer's right. "Stephan Svoboda, for whom do you vote?"

"Due to his unique role in our society and worldwide connections, I cast my vote for Ansen Clayborn."

Whew. Tied, one to one.

One after the other, votes were cast, the lead going back and forth between them. In the end, Charlotte and Zadie were the last two regular voters and would decide the race if they selected the same candidate. They didn't, as Charlotte continued the trend. "In these turbulent times I choose experience. I vote for Liza."

Crap.

It was Zadie's turn, and her eyes narrowed and shoulders rolled back subtly. Her words were deliberate and methodical. "Five years ago, I looked up to Liza as a mentor and considered her a friend... right up until the moment she tried to kill me and my unborn child." She breathed in deliberately. "Today, we may not always agree, but we've mended our relationship and work together for the good of our society." A stare swung between Ansen and Liza like a lighthouse beam. "But this vote is about who I trust at the helm and I don't believe it should even be close. Based on his bravery and respect for life... all life... I cast my vote for Ansen."

His nod toward Zadie was small. *Thank you, my friend. Now it all comes down to Imka... and unpredictability is her trademark. If she and Liza have a deal, this could be very bad.* With his hands below the table he crossed his fingers on both hands, then waited for the verdict.

Imka stood with her head high, as graceful as a warrior queen. "With such a close race, it is clear that we have two equally capable candidates ready to lead us into our glorious future." A serene gaze made its way slowly around the table. "As interim leader it now falls to me to cast the final vote."

Imka, what are you going to say next? He uncrossed, then re-crossed his fingers. *What's certain is I need to find out what Dr. Chavez knows, and the only way that's going to happen is if she chooses me. Come on, Imka!*

With the gaze of a judge handing down a verdict she looked toward Liza, then Ansen. "I respect experience, and admire bravery, so my decision has not been easy." Imka paused for several seconds staring straight ahead, as if torn, then her firm countenance eased into a smile and her eyes moved to the right. She spoke with fire and spirit. "It is with great pleasure that I introduce Ansen Clayborn as our next patriarch."

Relief swept over Ansen like a sudden cool breeze on a hot day as his fellow council members stood and clapped politely. His cheeks felt warm and he now joined them in standing. "Thank you all very much. It's a great honor."

Liza made her way around the table and offered her hand with a look he felt didn't fully match her words. "Congratulations, Ansen. It was a close vote, but the council has spoken. You can count on me for support, and I'll have your back in tough votes."

He returned a firm grip, chin held high. "Thanks, Liza. That means a lot." He hoped his smile appeared warmer than his thoughts. *I just hope you don't have a knife in your hand when*

DAVID WITT

you're standing behind me.

CHAPTER TWENTY-ONE

Maddy and Gwen had just started the seventh take recording their new duet when Gwen flubbed the words again. Maddy closed her eyes, her heart aching, as the producer cued up the music to start the eighth whenever the two women were ready. "Mom, we don't have to do this now. Maybe we take a break?"

Gwen's voice sounded weak and fearful. "Maybe for a few minutes, but that's all. If we don't get this track down today, I'm afraid I'll be even worse tomorrow."

Taking her mother's hand, Maddy guided her as they walked together toward the door that led to a sunbathed portico. "A little sunshine will do us both some good."

As they stepped through the door, Gwen stumbled, pulling them both down on the smooth concrete. "Damn it!" The weakness in Gwen's voice was replaced by loud anger as she yelled at no one in particular. "Somebody better fix that fucking door sill, or heads will roll!"

Looking back as she helped her mother up, Maddy couldn't see anything wrong with the doorway. *Shit, it's getting worse, fast.* "Don't worry mom, I'll have it taken care of ASAP."

"Good. Sometimes I think the people around here are trying to kill me."

The wild look in her mother's eyes scared Maddy. *Paranoid delusions too? Oh, God...* "We'll do background checks on everyone again. Let's just enjoy this day together, okay?"

Taking a seat on a comfy patio glider, Gwen seemed to calm as she squeezed her daughter's hand. "I know what's going on, and I hate it. It's just there's not a damn thing I can do about it."

Squeezing back, she answered softly. "Mom, dad's working on some new things, he's going to find a way to stop this. You'll see."

Wiping away a single tear, Gwen turned her face to the sun with eyes closed, as they sat side by side in silence. Uncounted seconds fell one by one into piles of quiet minutes. "Promise me you'll watch after your father after I'm gone."

"Mom, don't talk that way! You're not going anywhere for a long time." She said the words with as much sincerity as she could muster, even though she herself had more doubt than ever. "You have to believe."

A crinkled smile turned Gwen's words sunny. "I'm a fighter, baby girl. I might be going mad, but I'll not go quietly."

"That's the spirit." She gave her mom's hand a gentle tug. "Think you might be ready to give that song another go?"

"Abso-freaking-lutley! Let's do this!"

They walked back toward the studio with new energy, but Maddy still pointed to the door sill as they re-entered the building. "Watch your step."

Gwen did a little hop over the threshold, holding more tightly than ever, giggling like nothing had happened. When the door closed behind them, she turned to Maddy. "What song were we working on, anyway?"

CHAPTER TWENTY-TWO

Yesterday, Becky's temper had boiled over … again, this time directing her wrath at a coffee barista who made a mistake. *If I wanted fucking soy milk, I would have asked for fucking soy milk, you stupid steam head!* Recalling her words made her blush again. She had stewed in bitter anger in the days after her and Kelley's abduction, the threats against them causing her to explode more than once. She did her best to hide these displays, knowing how upsetting they would be to her wife. Failing to come up with any options for reprisal on her own, she pulled out her phone and scrolled through her contacts looking for her godmother's name. It had been years since they talked, and there was bad blood between them, but she felt cornered like a wild animal and needed to either vent or strike out at someone. This call would probably provide one of those outcomes. Hearing the woman's voice on the other end assured her that she had made a good choice.

"Becky? Is that you?"

While she knew that her father was already dead before Liza was offered the option to switch sides in the society civil war, her choice had never set well with Becky. She tried her best to delete the residual venom from her words. "How's life with the originals?" A few weeks ago, she would have added the word 'traitor' to the end of that sentence.

A long pause hung in the ether between them until the older woman spoke in flat tones. "It's been better. I don't know if you've heard, but Kristoff Svoboda is finally dead."

The message traveled halfway around the world, and then from Becky's ear to her brain in milliseconds, and suddenly her mood turned to euphoria. "Thank the Lord, I've been waiting for this day for years! I hope the bastard burns in hell for all the damage he caused." Then it dawned on her that Liza didn't sound nearly as happy as her. "What's wrong? Aren't you glad? That son of a bitch killed my father, and so many of our friends."

A sigh sounding of frustration landed before Liza's reply. "Don't get me wrong, I wasn't sad to see the old pig go, it's just that I had my sights set on replacing him. After all I've done, I deserved it. I know it's too late to completely stop designer babies, but I could have done so many other things of which your father would have been proud."

The mention of designer babies made Becky's skin crawl. "Speaking of those genetic mutants, that's why I called. I've had a very unpleasant run in with one of those test-tube freaks and it makes me want to puke. I felt dirty just being around them."

"I got a second-hand taste of that myself. The sperm donor for the first one of those abominations beat me in the election to succeed Kristoff. They picked that frat boy, Ansen Clayborn, over me! I'm disgusted."

Hearing the name 'Clayborn' brought her anger to full boil and spittle flew from her mouth as she spoke. "His evil spawn of a son is the one who's giving me problems! Maybe we can work together on our revenge. Dad always said payback is a bitch!"

Now the laugh she remembered so well came through the phone. "Your father was a wise and brave man who also knew how to turn a phrase. I'm tired of sucking up to these misguided shmucks. We might not be able to turn back the hands of time, but I'm positive that we can find ways to extract a measure of retribution for their actions, and perhaps give me another stab at taking over."

"I'm so glad I reached out to you. I feel so much better already!"

Liza sounded hopeful and full of promise. "I'll be in New York next week and we can toss some ideas around to make them pay."

"I would like that. I always hoped you weren't completely corrupted by those arrogant sons-of-bitches."

"It's been a hard five years." Liza sighed. "But now I know for sure I'll never get what I deserve unless I take matters into my own hands. Maybe this can be the start of a beautiful new partnership."

CHAPTER TWENTY-THREE

Adam waited impatiently for his parents to arrive back from Europe. Becky Brown had been very clear that they were hiding something from him, something big, and he wanted answers. When he arrived at their place, they were both staring at their computer screens, apparently very busy, but he was tired of waiting. With his mother back in the in-home office and father at the kitchen table on his laptop, he decided to start with him. *No beating around the bush, I deserve answers, now.* He sat down across the table. "Hey dad, what do you know about a man named Ben Brown?"

Fingers that had been striking the keyboard suddenly stopped, and a face like stone glared back. "Where did you hear that vile name?"

Guess I'm on the right track. He steadied himself as his father's face burned. "Well…" His voice cracked, nervous at confronting his father. "See, me and Ens and Maddy were pretty pissed off about getting attacked that night in Chalky's, so we decided to do a little digging."

His father's voice grew louder. "How many times have we told you the world is always watching you? What did you do?"

He felt his cheeks reddening like a rose blooming, not enjoying his father's hostile attitude. "The plan sounded good at the time." He fidgeted in his chair for a moment and his eyes cast down, suddenly feeling a little ashamed of how the women were snatched up and having to explain it to his father. "Turns out the goons were led by a woman named Becky Brown, his daughter." He shot a look at his father, trying to gauge his reaction.

Louder still, his dad questioned. "What did you do?"

Adam's fingers drummed on the table. "Well... the company we hired has special skills and they persuaded Becky and her wife to join us for a private meeting."

Ansen's eyes sprung open. "They kidnapped them! Is that what happened!"

"Not exactly... well, I mean... yeah, that's what you would call it." A memory of the night at Chalky's flashed, and he regained his footing, going back on offense. "After what they did to me, I felt completely justified. They had it coming, both of them. Becky Brown and her wife Kelley Slaughter."

Now yelling, his father exploded. "Please, tell me you didn't kill them."

"No!! Of course not. Why would you even think that?" His eyebrows arched as he remembered what they had done. "Although Maddy did rough one of them up, just a little, but no broken bones or anything. We wanted to let them know to leave us alone... or else." He drummed his fingers again and his head tilted. "And that's when things got interesting, and why I have some questions for you."

Bree came running into the kitchen. "What the hell's going on out here?"

Ansen motioned to the chair beside him. "I've just learned of some extracurricular activity by our son. It's time for an overdue family meeting."

Her eyes bounced between them. "Start again you two."

Ansen raised his index finger toward his son. "Tell your mom what you've been up to." Then he glanced at Bree. "You're going to *love* this."

Adam recounted what he had told his dad already, watching his mother appearing to grow more agitated, right up to the point of explaining how Maddy had roughed up Kelley.

Now it was she who blew a gasket. "What! That's not how we raised you to treat a woman, no matter what they might have done to you."

He shot back. "To be fair, it was Maddy who did that, not me."

"Grrr. You're missing the point. What you did is illegal, and could get you in serious trouble. You must have been thinking like the five-year-old you still are!"

"Hey! They're the ones who started this by attacking us, remember?" He caught his breath and tried to deescalate the situation. "And unless they're ready to implicate themselves in a worse crime than what we did to them, we're not in any legal danger." There was a moment of silence as he stared at them, now really ready to get answers. "Speaking of crimes, Becky Brown said you guys killed her father as well as her wife's father." He asked disbelievingly. "Is that true?"

His mother drew in a slow breath, gave a nod to his father, then answered. "I assume they left out the part about their fathers trying to kill me three times and your dad twice in the nine weeks I carried you?"

"What?" He couldn't believe the words coming from the mouth of his normal, planet loving mother. "What the hell are you talking about?"

He watched her head move slowly up and down. "They also attempted to murder Maddy's and Ensley's parents as well." Hearing sarcasm as thick as molasses added bite to what she said next. "Ben Brown, Ezra Slaughter? Those two men were a real barrel of monkeys, the life of the party. Their hatred of me as I carried you knew no bounds, and while neither your father or I pulled the triggers, they were killed to stop the ongoing threats to all of us."

Stammering, his voice raised. "Seriously, that really happened?" Thoughts bounced like ping pong balls. "Is that really true? Why didn't you tell me? Why did I have to learn this from strangers?"

His father stepped in. "Let's have some perspective here. You might be over six feet tall and a college graduate now running a successful business, but it's also a fact that technically you're only five-years-old. I know it's been tough for you, but it's been a blur for us as well. Time has been out of whack for us all, and it's things like this that got skipped."

He rubbed his head, still not sure if he was hearing the truth, but playing along for the moment. "Fair enough, I guess. But this seems pretty big." He crossed his arms and leaned back as his eyes narrowed, deciding to press again. "But now that we've opened this can, what else have my picture-perfect parents kept hidden? I want the whole story."

Shoulders slumping, his mother glanced at his father with what he interpreted as a look of resignation. "I guess it's time for the talk."

Feeling more in control of the situation, humor returned. "If this is about the birds and bees, save your breath. I know *all* about that."

There was no humor in his father's retort. "If only it were that simple."

The tone got Adam's attention. "Dad… what are you trying to say? Are you and mom in the mob?"

His parents looked at each other again before his father replied. "I'll start from the beginning." He glanced at her once more. "But feel free to jump in anytime."

"We'll tell him together."

Rolling up his sleeve, Ansen revealed his Tree of Life tattoo. "Have you ever wondered about my ink?"

"Not really. What is it?"

"The answer to everything." He stretched his arm out on the table. "This symbol means that I am a member of the Tree of Life Society, like my father and mother before... and like all of my direct ancestors for over six hundred years."

Adam's eyes darted fast between them. "What are you talking about? Mom, is dad messing with me? Seeing how far he can go before we all have a good laugh? Because if he is, it's not funny."

Her eyes looked concerned, not deceptive. "That's the way I felt when I found out about my ancestors. I didn't get the tattoo, but *both* branches of your family are part of a very ancient order."

"You two must think I'm stupid!" His palm slapped the table. "You're hiding something and this BS is the best you can come up with? I'm no fool!"

His mother reached for his hand and held it gently. "Adam, you're definitely not a fool. In fact, you might be the smartest person on the planet. Did you ever stop and wonder why you were the first genetically modified human? It wasn't by accident. Your birth was the culmination of a centuries long project."

Standing swiftly, he almost tipped the kitchen chair over as he shouted. "I came to you with serious questions, and this is the way you treat me? What kind of parents are you?"

In a low and steady tone, his father replied. "I know it's a lot to process, but we can prove everything we're saying."

Pacing the length of the open dining area and back, his mind raced. *Are they being serious? Trying to throw me off what's really going on? Straight out lying?* His hands landed hard on the table as he leaned toward his parents. "You can prove it, huh? Do it!"

Pulling her phone from her pocket, his mom spoke to him tenderly. "Call either of Ensley's parents, or Dr. Chavez. They're members too. They will be surprised to hear the question from you, but they will validate everything we've told you... and the things we're about to tell you."

Snatching the phone from her and feeling like he was still being lied to made his words taste bitter. "You think I won't do it, don't you?" He thrust the device back in her direction. "Unlock it!"

She pressed her thumb on the sensor, her voice just above a whisper. "Call all three, if it makes you feel better. We can give you more names, if you still don't believe us."

He stood with the unlocked screen glowing in his hand, frozen as he processed the possibility that she was telling the truth, until the glowing faded.

"Sweetie, do you want me to unlock it again, or would you rather ask us some more questions?"

Seeing their pained expressions, he realized they were telling him the truth. He mechanically handed her phone back. "Seriously?"

Both stood, then walked around the table, wrapping him in a loving family embrace until his father spoke. "We didn't expect to be having this talk today, but it's time. Let's have a seat and mom and I will tell you about your heritage, and answer all your questions. How's that sound?"

His reply was shaky. "For what it's worth, I didn't expect to find out today that my parents were in some secret sect like the Illuminati or Free Masons."

Laughing, his dad replied. "Hey! Don't insult us! We keep our secrets much better."

CHAPTER TWENTY-FOUR

The loud, caffeinated, chatty buzz of the coffee shop ensured that Becky and Liza's conversation wouldn't be overheard. Both of Becky's hands cupped around her cappuccino, nervous to be so close to a woman she had once admired, then despised. *Let's see where we stand now.* "The world has changed a lot for both of us in the last five years, hasn't it? Kelley and I are married and starting a family that would have gotten us excommunicated, or worse, and you're on the council of the originals. My father must be rolling in his grave."

The older woman almost spit out her sip of Caramel Macchiato as she contained a laugh. "You can't say something that funny when I have hot coffee in my mouth! I loved him like a brother, and I miss him, but he wasn't great at accepting change."

"That's the truth. Clearly, I disagree with him about his views on same sex marriage, but I still admired his passion and commitment to causes in which he believed, and I know how strongly you felt as well." Becky's amiable smile faded and her eyes hardened as she asked a question that had bothered her for a long time. "I know you faced a life or death choice to join those people, but how can you do their bidding every day, then sleep at night?"

Liza bowed her head, and her words sounded as if she were in a confessional booth bearing her soul. "The truth is I haven't had a truly good night's sleep since the night your father was murdered and I made the decision to save my life by switching sides.

I put on a brave face every day, hiding my true feelings. I've tried to convince myself that by living, I could make a difference working from the inside, and I have saved the lives of many from our side. But at what cost? More and more GM children are born every year and some of your father's dire predictions are starting to come true. Some nights I toss and turn wishing I had never been given a choice, just received the same fate as Ben."

Becky reached for Liza's hand, glad to hear Liza's decision to switch sides wasn't easy. *Maybe we can work together.* "You made the only choice you could. But now you have new options, and I think you're here with me today because you've already decided to change course. Am I right?"

The smile that stole onto the older woman's face indicated that she had indeed turned a page in her relationship with the society. "The first thing I want is revenge on that nasty woman, Imka Nkosi. That bitch cast the deciding vote selecting Ansen Clayborn as the next patriarch. Taking her out will shake up those council members, and be the first step on my path to get what I deserve."

Releasing Liza's hand, Becky did a double take, then spoke slowly, wanting to make sure she heard correctly. "Take her out? Are you serious?"

Liza nodded, then sounded as casual as if talking about hauling out the garbage. "Of course. Do you have a better way to take a measure of revenge and roil up that self-satisfied bunch?" Her serious look changed, as if understanding she might not be on the same page as Becky. "When we spoke on the phone, I understood you wanted to deliver some payback to the society. Did I misinterpret?"

Becky leaned forward and whispered in the loud room causing Liza to inch closer. "Payback, yes. I just didn't realize we would go from zero to murder right off the bat."

Liza sat up straight and folded her arms. "Are you sure you're

Ben Brown's daughter? He was a man who never shied away from doing what needed to be done, and I assumed you would be cut from the same cloth. I guess I was wrong."

The rage that was always just below the surface flared and Becky slammed a hand down on the table. "You better take that back, or we'll have a problem!" Everyone in the crowded room fell silent and Becky felt her cheeks warm. Glancing around, she saw all eyes on her. "Sorry, folks. Nothing to see." She gave a weak wave and one by one the gawkers went back to their own conversations.

A smirk accompanied Liza's reply. "At least you inherited his temper, it's the stuff of legend among old reformers. Everyone's got at least one story about Ben flying off the handle."

"One? I lived with him. I've got a thousand." Becky chuckled. "Look, you caught me off guard, that's all." *That, and the fact that I've never killed anyone. It's time to grow up, because I can't be a coward if I really want revenge. Now, just act like you know what you're doing.* "I knew taking on the originals was stepping up to the big leagues, it's just that I'm usually the one pushing others to the next level, not the other way around. What's the plan?"

The smirk eased into a cocky smile. "Imka's coming to the states next week, so we'll have home field advantage. It will be quick and clean. I'll have the final details ironed out later this week."

The combination of caffeine and the thought of working with Liza to begin wreaking havoc on the society equally energized and scared Becky, her thoughts skipping to the future like fast forwarding through commercials on a TV recording. "And after the Imka woman, we target one of those mutant twerps, right?"

A slow head-bob complimented Liza's smile. "I knew I was right. You *are* a chip off the old block."

Becky felt on top of the world hearing that compliment. "All I've ever wanted was to make him proud."

CHAPTER TWENTY-FIVE

In the days after meeting with Liza, Becky's mood improved dramatically and a visit to their obstetrician lifted it even further. "Maybe we'll find out if we're having a boy or a girl."

Kelley's blue eyes caught the sun as she looked up at Becky. "You know, we could have chosen, if we wanted."

A happy shrug telegraphed her answer. "I know, but everything else about invitro babies is so science based. I think it's a rush to leave it to chance, and I'll be just as thrilled with whatever we hear."

In short order they had checked in and been escorted back to an exam room where Kelley lay prone on a table. "I still can't believe our child is growing inside me. I almost tear up every time I stop and think about the miracle of life."

Becky held her hand as Dr. Simon entered speaking in her high soprano voice. "How is my patient today?"

"Happy, nervous, excited... maybe a little scared."

"All are completely normal emotions." The doctor stepped toward equipment just out of reach. "Unbutton your blouse and let's do an ultrasound to see if we can ease a little of the typical anxiety of first-time moms."

Doing as instructed, Kelley lay exposed as warm lubricating gel was applied to her skin. "We were wondering about the sex of the child. Will we find out today?"

Dr. Simon placed the listening part of the machine on her skin as she replied. "It's a little soon for that. Maybe next visit." Just then a womp-womp sound filled the entire room. "Hear that? It's your baby's heartbeat. Strong and clear."

Both mom's eyes filled as Becky now stood and leaned over in a hug with Kelley. "You're going to be a terrific mother."

"Let's take some measurements, okay?" The video screen part of the machine was positioned bedside. The doctor pointed with one hand as the other hand held the ultrasound device to Kelley's mid-section. "See? There's your baby."

The tears that Kelley had managed to hold now streamed from the corners of her eyes as she saw a tiny human with eyes, arms and legs. "That's amazing! Look, Becky! That's our baby!"

Becky wiped her eyes, holding back a full release. "Does everything look normal?"

"Let's take a closer look." Lines appeared on the screen as the doctor clicked. "The baby is a bit on the big side. Do either of you come from tall families?"

A smile bloomed on Becky's face as a memory of her father flashed in her mind. "Yes. My dad was a very large man. As big as a grizzly bear, God rest his soul."

"Then all looks like it should."

Becky beamed. "Thank you again, Dr. Simon. We wouldn't be here without all you've done. You're a miracle worker."

Dr. Simon pulled the machine back and handed Kelley some paper towels to clean the gel from her skin. "Don't give me too much credit. There's miracles and then there's science... and this is definitely science."

CHAPTER TWENTY-SIX

Adam arrived at Chalky's and Kiss Me Kimee led him to the VIP section. The bodyguard who now accompanied him on orders of his parents, followed several paces behind. Adam still enjoyed watching her rhythmically swaying hips as she walked, but the vibe from the last time he saw her had changed. It was clear in his mind that what they shared that night was fun, but it was a one-time thing... and he hoped she felt that way as well. "How's school?"

Her reply surprised him. "One of my professors hit on me today and I'm deciding how bad I need an 'A' in his class."

"Really?!"

"Just jokin'." She laughed. "I get my A's the old-fashioned way - by studying my ass off. Are you partying alone tonight or expecting company?"

Her laugh and joke put him at ease, and he read into it that she felt the same as he about their tryst. "Ensley should be here any minute. Oh, wait. I see her now." He waved and Ens waved back, now heading toward him, her own bodyguard in tow.

Kiss Me Kimee nodded. "I'll get her drink order on the way to the bar. What are you having tonight?"

"Maker's, on the rocks." With that she swished away, meeting Ensley halfway. The two women stood facing opposite directions triggering a thought. *Ens has always been a best friend... but when I think of her lately, I'm beginning to wonder if there can be more? Starting with what Kimee and I shared.* His mind shifted to the conversation they were about to have concerning the Tree of Life Society. *I still can't believe all this is true.*

She made her way to the private table and stuck her hand out. "Did your parents teach you the secret handshake?"

"What? There's more weirdness?"

She snickered. "Just messin'."

"For a half-second I thought you were serious." His chuckle was soft. "Maybe there is one, for all we know."

Kimee returned with the drinks as Ens took her seat. "An Appletini for the lady, and a Makers for the gentleman, compliments of Chalky." Without warning she leaned in and kissed Ensley. "That's compliments of me." She smiled a mischievous smile as she cocked her head. "You guys are welcome here anytime."

Ens sounded stunned as Kimee strutted away. "First, she kissed Maddy, now me. I guess you're next."

He shrugged, trying to maintain a straight face. "I bet she's a good kisser."

Ens nodded. "Yeah, she is. Guess that's how she got her name." She picked up her drink, raising it to toast. "To our strange lives."

"Amen to that." After clinking their glassware, they took their first sips, then Adam's voice lowered to just above a whisper. "So, how did your society talk go?"

Shaking her head in apparent bewilderment, Ens answered. "They kept talking and talking and all I could think was is this some kind of elaborate prank? Seriously, it seemed like aliens switched out my parents with body doubles."

"Utter disbelief." He took another sip. "Yet, as far as I can tell, it's all true. And we can't talk about it with anyone, even Maddy."

"That's the hardest part, for sure. It's like the three of us share everything, and now there's going to be this hidden thing between us. I don't like it one bit."

He cast her a curious glance. "What did they say about joining? Are you going to do it?"

She picked up her green drink and took a long sip, seeming to ponder her response. "They certainly leaned on me, but I didn't make a commitment. I don't know what to think."

Adam agreed. "Same here. Dad pushed more than mom, but they both made their points. They told me about the times they were attacked while they were expecting us, and linked it to the raid here, where I got hurt. They said these kinds of crimes are increasing around the world and the society could offer us full protection as members. I mean, if not for our rapid healing edit, I could have died."

Ensley visibly shivered. "Don't remind me of that night. I though we lost you and every few nights the whole thing replays as nightmares." She reached for his hand and her words sounded pained. "Losing you would break my heart."

Adam felt her hand squeeze his, and he liked it. His words tumbled from his heart as he looked into her sparkling dark eyes. "It will take more than some angry bitch to make that happen."

"So, you think we should join?"

"One minute I think, yes, then the next I think, no. Our lives are so freaking weird already, and joining a super-secret shadow organization sounds like another layer of stress I know I don't need."

Ensley's lips pulled thin. "But that WAGE group keeps stirring up trouble. Even if we blunt some of the laws they're trying to pass, they inspire extremists. Thanks to who we are, our future is only going to get more dangerous."

"Yeah, they've already passed that tax law on us, and the scholarship denial bill stands a good chance of passing. Just the debates about it will inspire the lunatic fringe."

"Their hatred isn't going away anytime soon and that's why my work is so important. Every day feels like a battle with life or death stakes."

She spoke the truth, and he knew it. His gaze now went over the crowded dance floor and to their armed protectors. "The threats are real, that's certain, but we have options. My parents told me about how they were brought into the fold, and for mom it was a negotiation, and we're in an even stronger position."

"Okay, I get it. And if we're united, we have even more power. Are you thinking what I'm thinking?"

Turning back to her, he winked. "We demand that Maddy be invited to join as well. We've been together all our lives and we're a package deal."

"I like that plan. How do you think they'll respond?"

His eyes widened. "Well, my father is the new patriarch, and from what I've picked up so far, that means he has a lot of power. It makes me optimistic."

Her face beamed. "The three amigos, always."

He stood, her hand still holding his. "Let's dance. It's a night to celebrate."

She quickly joined him, giving his hand another squeeze. "I like the way you think, and who knows, you might even get that kiss from Kimee tonight."

He shrugged. *This Kimee thing might not go away as easily as I hoped.* "Who knows?"

CHAPTER TWENTY-SEVEN

Becky was more nervous than the night she came out as gay to her grandmother. While that was a big deal, it wasn't criminal like what she was about to do. Her voice quivered as she spoke. "Can we go over the plan one more time?"

The question seemed to irritate Callan McDougal. "Look, you don't have to be here. In fact, you wouldn't be if Liza hadn't insisted."

Balling her hands into fists, Becky channeled her anger to help cover her nerves. "I'm here because that's the deal I made with her." She took a deep breath, then changed the subject, hoping to get on better terms with the leader of the hit team riding in a van through New York City. "I understand you knew my father, Ben Brown."

Callan's tone definitely changed. "He was a tough man, and a good man. Sorry about what happened."

With her jitters finally fully under control she responded. "I'm here tonight to get my first taste of payback. The woman we're targeting is part of the group that ordered his execution, so I hope you can understand why I insisted on being here."

The former special ops soldier grunted. "Uh ha. I get it. I would feel the same way." He leaned back, seeming a bit more relaxed. "Like I said, it's a pretty simple operation. We're doing a basic snatch-and-grab. After we have her in the van, we put a bullet through her brain before we get to the next block, then we dump her body at a secluded place down by the river. You'll be home before you know it."

Becky kept her composure as she recalled the night she and Kelley were the victims of a snatch-and-grab. When she thought about how quickly they had lost control of their lives it made her queasy. She had been terrified then, but put up a tough façade now as she prepared to do the same thing to another woman. "She deserves what's coming to her, but I'm glad she won't suffer."

He nodded agreement, glancing at the crew in the crowded van. "Same here. We've got a job to do, but we're not sadists."

You're going to kill a woman in cold blood. What do you call it?

The driver called from the front. "The spotter says she's left the hotel on foot, just like our source said she would. Are we still a go?

His answer was final. "We have a hard green on this job. No over-rides."

More info was relayed by the driver. "Target in sight with a clear sidewalk. Ready on my count in five, four, three, two, one. Now!"

Becky was amazed at the speed the team operated. In less than five seconds the side door opened and two soldiers jumped out, sweeping Imka Nkosi off her feet, then shoving her into the van. The door slid closed in a hurry and the van was already turning on a side street following the planned serpentine path toward the dump zone. No one on the team said a word as duct tape was stretched over Imka's mouth, muffling the panicked screaming. Zip ties quickly bound her, and in under fifteen seconds she was tied up and gagged, face down on the floor of the vehicle, being driven through the city toward her final destination.

Callan put his knee on the target's back to limit her desperate squirming. He took a pistol with a silencer out of a case and held it in an offering toward Becky. "Would you like to do the honors?"

This was the moment she knew was coming, the moment she had dreamed of for so long. But now that it was here, her emotions were not what she expected. She reached for the gun, then pulled her hand back. *I can't do this.* The tremble in her voice returned. "I think I'll leave this to the pros."

He shrugged, as if what he was about to do were just another Tuesday in the office. "As you wish."

The sound of the gunshot was muffled and Imka's body immediately went limp. Once again, the van was still and silent until new information was called out by the driver. "We'll be at the drop site in ten minutes."

Becky's insides went cold. *Oh...my...God. That really just happened.*

Handing the weapon to one of the team members, Callan gave an order. "Make sure this gets destroyed."

Becky's mind fractured and ricocheted as the scent of freshly spent gunpowder filled the small space. *I thought this would be different.... But she deserved it after what she did to my father.... What am I doing here???? Those freaks are ruining our world.... This could have happened to Kelley and me....* She looked directly at Imka's lifeless face; eyes open in a vacant stare. *What have I done?*

Soon the van slowed. "ETA in thirty seconds."

When the wheels stopped turning, the team again moved with precision and speed. The door opened and the fetid smell of mud from the river bank rushed in, adding a new aroma to the palate. They pulled her body out and tossed it like a sack of potatoes, which landed with a sickening thud in the wet muck.

The complete stop lasted less than thirty seconds and they were on their way back to mid-town. With the job done, Callan seemed to pivot his thoughts to the future. "Glad you joined us, Becky. That went exactly as planned. You're a lucky charm."

Her cheeks went hot as the blood rushed, not feeling exactly lucky at the moment. "I'm not sure about that. Your team seems pretty good at what they do."

"That's true, but I've been on enough jobs that have gone sideways that I'll take any luck I can get. I hear we'll be doing more of these kinds of contracts in the future." He patted her arm. "You remind me of your pops."

She hoped her fake smile didn't give her away. "Thanks for the invite, that means a lot." *Maybe I'm not as much of a daddy's girl as I thought.*

CHAPTER TWENTY-EIGHT

Ansen was directing movers unloading the furniture sent from their New York City apartment to their estate near the New York and Connecticut state line. The new digs were required to house the security details and other assorted necessities that coincided with his elevation to patriarch. His phone rang and he saw his wife's name. "Hey, Bree. What's up? Anything left to move from the old place?"

"Turn on the TV." Her voice cracked, as if she had been crying. "Something terrible has happened."

Turning in a complete circle, all he saw were boxes yet to be unpacked. "It's going to take a while to find a TV. What's wrong, I'll watch whatever it is on my phone as soon as we hang up."

"It's Imka." A moan accompanied her next words. "She's dead... murdered."

A massive sinking feeling consumed Ansen's entire body and a jumble of questions flowed. "What? Are you sure? What happened?"

Bree sniffed, then continued. "It's on the morning news. They found her body beside the river, just outside the city. She's dead... they say a single gunshot to the head. This is just awful."

Ansen glanced around until he found a sofa not covered in boxes and sat down. "I feel sick. I've got to contact Arnold and give him the bad news, if he doesn't know already." His mind flashed to just over a week ago when he saw the elegant couple in

Prague. "This can't be happening."

"I know your day just got turned upside down, so I'll call Adam and make sure he's safe and warned to be on guard. I'm going to insist he come out to the new place, at least for a day or two."

Ansen rubbed his forehead. "And now I'll definitely be on society business all day." Leaning back on the soft cushion he let out a slow breath. "So much for my honeymoon as the new patriarch."

"Good luck, Honey. I'll be there as quickly as I can."

As soon as the call disconnected, Ansen sent both texts and emails to the council members with the few details he had learned from Bree, then scheduled a video conference for later. His body tensed as he thought about what he needed to do next. Taking a calming breath, he called Imka's husband. Hearing Arnold's sobs, his heart broke.

"How did this happen?" Arnold demanded.

"We'll get to the bottom of this, I promise."

"I don't know how I will live without her."

A soft moan of grief reached Ansen's ear. "I can't imagine how you must feel. I'm so sorry."

Arnold whispered, sounding emotionally spent. "She was my soulmate."

"Our heart grieves with you, my friend. We will be by your side in this trying time." Ansen spent the remainder of the call mostly listening to the distraught man, comforting him when he could and promising they would find out who did this.

After the emotional call, Ansen walked outside for some fresh air and to get his emotions back under control. *Pull it together, there's a lot to do today.* Calmer, his next action was to place a call to Sameer Raj. His mind wandered as he waited to connect. *I know he voted for Liza instead of me, but he's old guard and knows all of our police contacts.*

Sameer answered with a catch in his voice. "H-Hello, Ansen. I just got your messages. I can't believe what happened."

"Yeah, I'm stunned, too, and it was a tough call to Arnold." *I can't linger there, I've got to shift gears.* "Right now, we need to find out if this was some random act of violence, or the first shot in a new war we weren't expecting."

He sounded surprised. "Do you really think that's possible? I mean, if this were five years ago, I would automatically assume it was the work of the reformers, but that threat is over. Who else could it be?"

"I hope you're right, but until we know, everyone needs to review their safety protocols and stay on alert."

The older man's words sounded as if he had now moved past shock and into action mode. "Agreed. I'll start working our contacts and find out what the police are thinking."

"Good, and keep me updated on anything you find."

"Absolutely." There was a pause, then Sameer continued. "I didn't vote for you, Ansen, but that doesn't mean I don't think you're up to the job. In fact, I think your decision-making history when under fire bodes well in this uncertain time. Just know that I've got your back on the council."

Ansen felt the sentiment was sincere. "I appreciate that." His thoughts went to the attack on Adam. "Based on the events of the past few weeks, I'll need it. I have a feeling we might be back at war again. I just don't know with whom."

CHAPTER TWENTY-NINE

Liza joined the afternoon video call with the council with three main objectives. The first was simple – act as sad as everyone else about Imka's death. There could be no hint of how excited she was at the success of this first attack. Secondly, she wanted to gain as much information as possible about clues, theories or suspects. It thrilled her to be on the inside while at the same time, calling the shots on taking this council down. Lastly, whenever possible she intended to sow seeds of doubt or provide false information to derail any investigation that was on the right trail. She had seen what happened to Ben and Ezra, and knew that would be her fate as well, if caught.

Ansen had just finished a touching memorial for Imka. "Would anyone else like to say a few words before we get down to the necessary business?"

Time to perform. "I knew her for less time than others, but in that short while, we formed a strong bond as mature female leaders of our society. Her spirit will stay with me forever." After attending so many funerals of fallen comrades, the gloomy expression Liza had perfected made the platitudes that flowed through her lips sound convincing.

Ansen directed the call as if he had been the patriarch for years, no nerves apparent on his first global meeting. "Thank you, Liza. Would anyone else like to say a few words?"

Liza maintained a sphinxlike expression as one by one they all spoke of a memory or two of the long serving member. *Who's the next target. It needs to be someone who really supports Ansen. When he's isolated and weak, I'll take him down and assume my rightful place. Hmmm, let's see.* Then her eyes landed on the square containing Zadie's image. *There's the winner. Her betrayal is what triggered the fall of the reformers in the first place. Payback's going to be fun with that one.*

When everyone finished, Ansen transitioned to the parts of the call in which Liza was most interested. "Initial indications are this was a professional hit. Not a random act of violence. I've asked Sameer to brief us on what we know so far."

Putting reading glasses on, Sameer glanced at what appeared to be hand written notes. "We have a source in the NYPD and he has access to the electronic database. So far they are thinking the same as us." He took in a deep breath, then cleared his throat. "Sorry everyone, this is tough to read about one of our own." His head tilted slightly as he continued. "Imka's body was found on the banks of the Hudson, face down in mud, with her hands and feet bound."

Grumbling traveled through the fiber optic connections at light speed, broken only by Liza's self-muffled gasp. "I'm sorry. That's just an awful thing to have happened." What she failed to mention was that Callan had sent an encrypted photo of the scene to her yesterday, giving her great satisfaction.

Sameer continued. "Her purse, wallet and phone were found with her, and none of her jewelry had been removed. This was definitely not a robbery gone bad."

Ansen seemed all business now. "Do they have any evidence, leads, theories?"

"Here's what they know so far." Sameer looked down again at his notes. "At the dump site they have a few footprints of identical sport shoes, all in the same size. They think this might be a ploy to confuse any investigation of the attackers. If this was done by pros, those shoes have already been burned."

Liza resisted the urge to smile. *So far so good. No real clues.*

He flipped the page on a yellow legal pad. "They found a burned-out van abandoned in New Jersey, and looking at traffic cam footage near Imka's last known location, they're almost positive it was used in her abduction. They're processing the vehicle, but don't expect much."

Callan seems to have really delivered.

Flipping one more page, Sameer gave the synopsis. "As far as theories or suspects, the police are in the dark right now. They're actively working the case, but at this time they're nowhere."

"That's what I expected." Ansen's face hardened. "Tell me *we* have some suspects."

Sameer's head lowered. "We're in the same place as the NYPD."

"Anyone else care to weigh in on suspects?"

Stephan Svoboda chimed in from Prague. "It's been five years since the fall of the reformed movement. Maybe a disgruntled faction has banded together to seek revenge?"

Ansen nodded, then stared at his screens.

Did his eyes just glance at my image? Stop it, Liza, you're being paranoid.

Looking into the camera, Ansen questioned. "Liza, you have a lot of contacts in the old faction. Have you heard rumblings out there? Has anyone who was left behind reached out to you?"

This wasn't her first rodeo, so her face didn't flinch, nor her voice change. "I haven't heard a thing, but if you would like I can make a few inquiries."

His answer was delayed by a few seconds, as if he was processing her reply. "Yes. But do it on the downlow. We don't want to tip our hand or give anyone not involved any new ideas."

She smiled and nodded. "I'll make the calls ASAP." Her smile lingered. *These young guns are smarter than I thought, and Ansen's performing better under pressure than I anticipated, but they're no match for me. I was running operations when they were still in diapers.*

Glancing at his newly installed office screen, Ansen continued, addressing another member. "Zadie, would you remind everyone of level five security procedures? It's been a while since it's been this high."

His friend and fellow designer baby parent took over. "If you live in an area of the world where permanent protection details aren't needed, please activate your contingency plan. If someone's hunting us, no need to make it easy."

Speaking of easy, Callan's next job won't be as simple.

Zadie continued the security portion of the call. "And if you have children or grandchildren... especially one of our special children, you should increase their protection as well. We're all aware of the threats they already face, and until we know more we have to assume it's increased."

Oh yeah, those little monsters. Becky wants to target one of them next.

Ansen resumed control of the virtual meeting. "Arrangements for Imka's funeral in South Africa are being made as we speak. I'm assuming most of us will attend, but we need to invoke the Designated Survivor protocol." His eyes seemed to scan each of the images of the members on his screens. "Charlotte, I know you and Imka were close, but I'm asking that you stay home in case a mass attack occurs."

She nodded into the camera from her home in Sydney Australia. "I wish it weren't necessary, but I understand. Would you please deliver my condolences to Arnold?"

Good! She voted for me and she's guaranteed to be safe, if I were to decide to go for all the marbles at one time.

"Certainly. I'm sure he will understand your absence." Ansen's tone changed. "Remember, everyone, our society has faced plagues, civil war, and even other assassinations in our long history. Like today, those were dark times, but we've always persevered, coming out the other side stronger. Rest assured, we'll do the same again. Let's all stay safe as we continue building a better world."

Liza's mournful visage remained until the meeting ended and the cameras turned off. *I can't believe I've put up with this crap for five long years, and good luck with staying safe. I have plans to ensure that doesn't happen.*

CHAPTER THIRTY

Adam had received the call about the death of Imka Nkosi from his mother and been given firm orders to go to their new home. *Good, I need to talk to them anyway.* Traffic was light and he arrived in just under an hour. Aside from the country setting and size of the estate, the main thing he noticed was the presence of security guards everywhere, including the two at the gatehouse. *Guess dad's new gig is a bigger deal than I realized.*

He was met at the door by a rather large muscular man dressed in a commando style black uniform who greeted him by name. "Mr. Clayborn, your parents are expecting you. Please, follow me to the library."

Yeah, way bigger.

Bree spotted him first and embraced her full-grown son in a bear hug. "Thank God you're safe!"

Ansen stood from his desk and joined them. "Glad you got here so quick. We still don't know the extent of the threat."

Adam sensed their tension. "You think we're in danger?"

"Sorry about the mess in here. A crisis in the middle of a move is not the way I wanted to start my new role." Ansen motioned toward two arm chairs not covered in boxes or packing material. "Have a seat and we'll bring you up to speed."

Adam's stomach had settled on the ride out, but hearing the grizzly details of Imka Nkosi's murder triggered unease again. "And you think whoever did that to her might come after us?"

Ansen's hands went out to his sides. "That's the thing. We just don't know, but with all we've been through, we've learned it's better to be safe than dead."

The word 'dead' registered like a slap to the face, causing Adam's eyes to widened. "Who do you think did it? Could it be connected to Becky Brown and her bunch of goons?"

Bree entered the discussion forcefully. "Let me make one thing clear, young man! You stay away from her, she's bad news. Besides, this is Tree of Life business, and we have resources and abilities to handle situations like this."

Adam looked around the stately room with leaded glass windows inviting views of rolling manicured fields, complete with guards on sentry duty. "Looks like you certainly do." He shook his head at the new environment around him. "I still don't quite believe all this, but it's getting more real every day. When you told me about it, I pictured kind of a boutique operation, seeing this I know I need to expand my mindset."

Ansen shrugged. "Yes, it's very real, and these resources could very well save your life." He paused for a moment as he glanced at Bree, then back to his son. "Speaking of the society, have you given any thought about a decision to join?"

Feeling nervous about the subject, Adam stood and slowly walked a few paces before answering. "That's been on my mind. I've talked it over with Ensley, and we have a request, actually more of a demand, before we commit."

His father's furrowed brow told Adam he probably struck a nerve. "If you haven't noticed, now isn't a good time to start a negotiation. Besides, that's not how this is usually done."

"But, Dad! Just hear me out."

Bree interrupted. "Let's hear what he has to say. If you recall, you and I had some serious discussions with Kristoff before my initiation."

"Thanks, mom." He stretched his open hands toward them.

"Here's the thing. From the beginning, Ens, Maddy and I have all been in this together. We don't think it's fair for us to join without including Maddy. That's what we want, we're a package deal." The two parents exchanged glances and he wasn't sure who would speak first, but considered it a good sign his demand wasn't shot down immediately.

Ansen tilted his head. "We understand where you're coming from, but it's not that easy."

Frustrated, Adam sounded off. "You're the head honcho of this shadow organization who's talking about the 'resources' and 'abilities' at your command, and you can't extend an invitation to a new member? Someone who is probably just as at risk as Ens and me? That's bull crap."

Lowering his voice, Ansen spoke slowly. "First of all, we care about Maddy, too. We think of her as family, so we can definitely offer protection, as we did for her parents five years ago. But membership is a whole different subject."

Hearing his father responding calmly and including an offer of protection, Adam sat back down. "I don't understand. It's not like we're a different species or something. Doesn't the group want fresh blood sometimes?"

Bree touched her son's hand. "Of course, new outsiders are brought in on a regular basis, and under normal circumstances she would be a great choice. It's just that, like her mother, it seems she shares every thought in her head with the world. I love Gwen like a sister, but that's why an invitation was never extended to her and Ray. We're a secret organization who does great things, but exposure could literally trigger wars. It's too big of a risk."

Adam sat silently for a few seconds with his head lowered, not wanting to fight with his parents, but not ready to give up either. Raising his head, he stared defiantly. "You saw how quickly I healed from that head wound, right?"

They both nodded.

"Well, did you know I probably can't drown?"

Their jaws fell open as they answered in unison. "What?"

"Yeah, that is if I have the same modifications as Maddy. She fell in the pool when she was a kid, and no one noticed for a long time. After her parents freaked out, they made her promise not to tell, and she hasn't told anyone except Ens and me. She can keep a secret."

Ansen rubbed his forehead. "That's certainly news to us. You've made a good point. Maybe you should have gone into law, like your mother."

As all three had a chuckle at the joke, knowing how Adam had fought that idea all through college. He was glad the tension was broken. "Will you at least think about our request. This means a lot to us."

Ansen stood and walked closer. "I promise we'll consider it, but right now we need to focus on this immediate threat. Mom and I will reach out to Ray and Gwen and offer help to their family if they need it, while only telling them what they need to know. In the meantime, how about I have Tilda show you to your suite here. Your mom and I think it's a good idea for you to hang out here for a couple of days until we have a better handle on what's going on. Maybe we'll even have a skeet shooting contest between the three of us."

"Sounds good, but we both know mom's going to win."

There was more laughter as the young man sauntered out of the library, finding a waiting Tilda outside the door.

When he was sure Adam was out of earshot, Ansen turned to Bree with a worried stare. "What do you make of that drowning story?"

"I mean, we can't be completely surprised after what we've already seen, can we?"

Touching his chin, his gaze went to the window and the rolling hills beyond. "With all that's happened in his short life, it's a wonder he's as normal as he is. You've done a great job raising him."

Bree moved beside him and put her arm around her husband's waist. "We've always made a good team, but I could use a stress break."

Ansen looked around at the moving mess as he pulled her closer. "That's just not going to happen. A council member was murdered and a world-wide group is working day and night to make our son a second-class citizen." An almost physical force seemed to weigh on his shoulders. "Then there's this thing with Chavez."

"Do you think things like that drowning story are part of the information she's going to tell us?"

"Maybe." He kissed the top of Bree's head. "Wonder what else we don't know about our boy?"

CHAPTER THIRTY-ONE

Becky and Kelley sat close together in a quiet corner of the waiting room at the clinic. Becky was anxious. "I hate when doctors run behind."

Kelley reached for her wife's hand. "She's not that late." Her hand gripped a little tighter. "Are you okay? You've seemed bothered by something these last few days."

"I'm fine." Becky's words were sharp and clipped. *Come on, pull it together, she doesn't need any more stress in her life.* "There's just a lot going on right now."

Nodding, Kelley rested her head on Becky's strong shoulder and whispered. "I know Phillip's bugging you to do another raid, but I worry about his stability. He had a lot harder time getting off drugs than you, and I suspect he might be dabbling again."

"Yeah, but it could just be his psych meds need adjusting."

Kelley shifted position. "After what happened with those freaks, we know we can't be doing anything like that right now. We have a baby on the way, and they specifically called out Phillip's name as a target if we try anything. We can't put him in danger."

Pulling their clasped hands up, Becky delivered a soft kiss to the back of Kelley's. *She can never find out what's really bothering me because she would never forgive me, and that would be worse than dying.* "Yeah. Only the public WAGE campaigns, otherwise I'm on the straight and narrow from here on out."

The nurse called their name and soon Kelley was reclined with her belly exposed. Dr. Simon maneuvered the ultrasound unit bedside as she entered. "How have things been going for you two since your last visit?"

Kelley smiled with dimples now appearing on her cheeks. "I understand all those jokes about pregnancy and eating. I'm always hungry and the pounds seem to be piling on."

Glancing at the electronic record, the doctor replied. "You're certainly gaining weight, but you're just barely above normal range. Keep an eye on your diet and add a few steps each day and you should be fine. Anything else?"

In a shaky voice, Becky asked the question that had been on their mind since their previous visit. "Some of our friends have commented on how big Kelley looks. We're anxious about today's ultrasound."

Dr. Simon's smile was broad and comforting. "I understand. Kelley is a petite woman, so that makes her baby bump look bigger than it really is. Besides, every pregnancy is different, and as I mentioned last visit, she is carrying a large child. Let's take a look."

The gel was applied and just a few seconds later they were staring at a smiling fetus. Kelley's tears immediately flowed. "That's our baby!"

Moving the device on Kelley's stomach, Dr. Simon asked a question. "Do you want to know the sex, or do you want to be surprised."

The mothers looked at each other and answered excitedly in unison. "We want to know."

"Alright then, let's see if I can get a good angle." The doctor rolled the device a few centimeters at a time until she got the ideal position. The image was unmistakable. "You're having a baby boy."

Becky joined Kelley in the tear brigade. "You don't know how happy that makes us." She rubbed her wet cheeks with the back of her hands. "We have already decided on a boy name. We're naming him after both of our fathers."

Dr. Simon's smile never faded as she adjusted the device to once again feature the angelic face of their soon-to-be born child. "That's so sweet. What's his name?"

Kelley stared intently at the image. "His name is Benjamin Ezra. We're still deciding if we're going with hyphenated last names or not."

"Awe, that's a strong name. You two are going to be such good parents."

Breaking her stare at the monitor, Becky checked back on her question. "So, I take it everything still looks normal?"

Dr. Simon handed Kelley tissues to wipe away the gel, then began putting the machine away. "Get ready for more stares when you're out and about, because this is a big boy, but other than that everything appears normal."

Becky helped Kelley stand after she got her clothing readjusted. "With everything that's going on in the world of babies these days, the word 'normal' is music to our ears."

CHAPTER THIRTY-TWO

This time Liza set up the meeting with Becky in a private location. Imka's death had raised alarm bells and she couldn't risk being seen with Ben Brown's daughter. What the cramped office in a hangar at the Morristown New Jersey airport lacked in ambience, it made up for in privacy. "Callan says you did great on your first job. How did it feel to rid the world of one of the people who killed your father?"

Becky bit her lower lip and sounded edgy. "The experience was almost surreal. I waited five years to see one of them pay the ultimate price, but I was more nervous than I let on. Callan and his team are real pros."

Liza had wanted to get revenge for Ben's murder for a long time, and it felt good giving Becky the same satisfaction. "It's time to build on the success of your maiden mission and take out one of those first three genetic modified scum. We might not be able to eliminate them all, but we can send a message. None of those freaks should ever feel completely safe."

Fidgeting hands accompanied a less than enthusiastic response. "I would like nothing better, but…"

"But what? You're the one who wanted to target one of them next?"

Becky's black Doc Martin boot slid back and forth on the smooth concrete floor. "Don't get me wrong, I'd like nothing better than to end all three of them today. It's just that Kelley's pregnant, and I don't want to do anything to jeopardize her, or our child." Her voice brightened. "By the way, it's a boy and we're going to name him Benjamin Ezra."

Liza's spirits soared upon hearing the choice. "Oh Becky, that's a wonderful name. I'm sure your fathers would be proud."

Becky's cheeks turned a rosy pink. "I hope so. The old reformers weren't keen on same sex marriage, but we're very happy."

"And you should be. Unadulterated children are our true legacy and I'm sure he would have come around sooner or later." Liza patted Becky's shoulder. "I wish you all the best, but I hope you understand, we're moving forward with the plan. Working from the inside failed, so I have a new mission, and I haven't felt this alive in a long time."

"Yes, by all means, proceed." She sighed and her tone darkened. "I really wish I could be part of the next operation, especially if it's that Blaze girl. I would pull the trigger on that bitch myself."

"Then maybe you'll reconsider, because she's the target. She's shooting a music video in Harlem tomorrow afternoon and Callan has everything all set. It's a simple drive by. In and out in less than thirty seconds." Liza locked eyes on Becky, looking like an alcoholic who had just been offered a shot. "What do you say?"

"Well..." Becky slowly shook her head and started again. "I can't be involved. It's too risky."

Liza's words coaxed, wanting to draw Becky closer into her orbit for future missions. "Callan says it's an even cleaner job than the last one."

The older woman could see the walls of resistance beginning to crumble as Becky licked her lips and her shoulders tensed. "Well...it was a rush seeing Callan and his men work...and Kelley will be leading a budget meeting, which I always skip..." She cracked her knuckles and her knee bounced. "I mean if Callan thinks it's safe, that we won't be found out... I... I really do owe that no talent skank a little something special."

"So, you're in?"

Becky took a deep breath and stepped over the edge, her words low and angry. "She hurt Kelley, and I can't forgive that. I'm in."

Liza's lips curled at the ends. "Your father would be so proud."

Her head bowed. "That's all I ever really wanted."

CHAPTER THIRTY-THREE

Maddy spoke to the stylist as finishing makeup touches were applied. "I'm glad I don't live a nine-to-five life. What Ens and Adam do is important, but also seems really boring."

Darla added her last flourishes. "You're ready, Mrs. Blaze. I'll be here when it's time for the wardrobe change."

Famed director, Xena Lombardi, welcomed Maddy to the street set in a sexy ninja outfit. "This will be nothing like your previous videos. It will be gritty and rough, and I guarantee it will rack up millions of views."

Punching one of the male backup dancers lightly on the arm, Maddy riffed. "I've been waiting for the right song to show off my martial arts skills, and *Fighting With My Nightmares* is perfect."

With the call of "action" by Xena, filming began with Maddy hitting every mark on the first take. Unfortunately, one of the dancers landed awkwardly after bouncing on a hidden mini-trampoline and crashed into another dancer. "Cut! Come on, guys. Be the pros that I know you are. Great job, Maddy. Now, let's take it from the top."

After four hours of filming the first scene, the director was satisfied. "Great job, everyone. Take a break and grab some dinner. We start again in an hour." She turned to the head of security. "Let the food trucks in."

Maddy spoke to an assistant as she walked toward the stylist.

"That was fun, but I'm starved. Grab me some Thai food."

She took three more steps, then heard shouts and gunfire. Spinning around, she felt a sting in her right shoulder, then a punch in the gut immediately followed by a sharp pain in her left leg that dropped her to the ground. Time seemed to slow down as she sought to make sense of what was happening. In the millisecond between blinks she understood the gravity of the situation. *I've been shot.*

The rate of shots being fired increased as she lay bleeding on the street, blood now trickling past her cheek which was flush with the grimy pavement. *I have to move!* Trying to push off the ground, her right arm proved useless. *Shit, this is bad.* Finally, she summoned enough strength to raise up on her left elbow, finding she could push with her right leg, moving her injured body in a slow army crawl. A chip of pavement bounced up beside her, stinging her side. *That was close. Got to keep moving.*

Darla suddenly appeared in front of her on her hands and knees, grabbing her under her armpits and dragging her away from the sound of violence. "Sorry if this hurts."

"Just keep pulling!" She felt a slam to her right calf. "Go, go, go!!"

Sirens closed in on their location, and tires screeching away coincided with the ceasing of gunfire. Darla dragged Maddy behind the base of a motorized camera boom and rolled her onto her back, the fear in her voice evident. "You're bleeding ma'am." Her head jerked, looking for something or someone. "Help! Anybody?? Help!"

With the sound of gunfire now gone, a new kind of noise erupted, a mix of desperation and chaos. Maddy felt light headed and grabbed Darla, who continued to beg for help on the set that now truly resembled a nightmare. "Darla, listen to me." She gasped for air, feeling her heart racing. "I need my phone." Another gasp, then a command with as much force as she could muster. "Now!"

The tone and directness must have worked, because it broke Darla's hysteria. "You want your phone?"

"Get it, now!" She felt her breathing becoming shallow. "Hurry!" Darla's eyes bulged and for a moment she seemed frozen in place. Maddy cursed. "Damnit, Darla. Go before I die." That did the trick as the stylist startled, then ran back to the dressing area.

Laying by herself she heard cries calling for help all over the ravaged set. Rather than upsetting her, in a perverse way she felt calmer, because she could feel that her body already responding, surely differently than the others injured as badly, or worse than her. *God help the others.*

Her breathing had steadied by the time Darla returned with her phone. Reaching out with her good hand she demanded the device. "Give it to me, then go help someone else. I'll be okay."

Darla's mouth hung open. "But ma'am, you've been shot. I need to help, somehow."

Maddy needed some privacy for this call and didn't have time to argue. Growing up the daughter of Gwen Blaze had taught her how to string together curse words. "God damn it, Darla. Fucking listen to me. Those sons-of-bitches hurt a lot of our people and I'm sure as hell others need the help far more than me. Now, go!"

Darla's body shook, but she stood and looked around at the chaotic scene. "I'll go find a paramedic."

With that, she was off, giving Maddy time to make the call she knew she needed to make. *Please answer.* As soon as she heard the click of an answer she started talking. "Listen to me, Adam. I need your help."

"Sure. What's up?"

Her speech was clear and direct. "I've been shot and I need you to meet me at the hospital."

His casual tone turned urgent. "Are you okay? Tell me you're alright!"

She looked down and saw blood staining her clothing in several places. "It's not pretty, but I'm already feeling better... if you know what I mean. I need you to meet me at the hospital and get me out of there as soon as possible."

"Yes... I understand." His voice trailed off and she knew he received her message.

Her mind was now completely clear as she gave more direction. "I'll have my stylist call you on this phone as soon as I know where they're sending me."

"Got it. I'll be there as fast as I can."

Another thought came to mind. "Oh, and Adam, you better bring your mom. I don't mean to scare you, but the way I look, it might take a lawyer to get me out of there."

CHAPTER THIRTY-FOUR

Two days after the attack on Madeline Blaze, everyone on the council other than Charlotte, was in Cape Town, South Africa for the memorial service and burial of council member Imka Nkosi. While neither Maddy Blaze nor her family were Tree of Life members, all knew the linkage and understood the significance of the attempt on her life. After the memorial service and burial, an impromptu meeting was called. For Liza it was another opportunity to spy from the inside.

Ansen began the meeting by saying what most had come to believe. "We're at war."

Master Fong asked the obvious next question. "Do we know our enemy?"

Ansen gave a short head shake. "Unfortunately, no." He pointed. "Sameer, please update us on this latest incident."

The man who was usually quick with a joke began his report with hard numbers. "Two days ago, eight people were killed and thirty wounded when a group of assassins drove onto Madeline Blaze's music video shoot. She was among the injured. The perpetrators stole a food truck three days earlier and outfitted it as a killing platform. The security personnel onsite were blindsided, and barely mounted a response before the assailants sped away. It was found burned to a crisp by a fire suspected to have been set with high temperature accelerants in an area with no cameras. The NYC police continue to work the case."

Liza listened intently. *So far nothing that I don't already know. Excellent.*

"Ansen," Zadie asked. "How is Maddy?"

"Initial reports were that she was gravely injured and near death, but those accounts were greatly exaggerated by the paparazzi. In fact, she was released from the hospital after a few hours, and is recuperating with her family as guests in my home. We have a long history, as you know."

Liza's expression remained unchanged as she listened to the hard to believe information. *How can that be? I saw video from Callan, and she was hit at least three times by high caliber ammo. Any normal person would be dead, or fighting for their life. There's more to this story and in time, I'll find out.*

Stephan Svoboda asked the next question. "Are we sure this is a war on the society, that these attacks are even connected?"

Sameer spoke up. "That's a valid question and we can now say with certainty that they are connected. Analysis of recovered bullets indicate that at least some of them were fired from the same weapon used in Imka's murder."

Liza didn't so much as flinch as she fume inside. *Sloppy! I paid top dollar to do this the right way. No weapon should ever be used twice!*

She was still hot when Ansen surprised her. "Now that we know the attack on Madeline Blaze is connect to Imka's death, we can say that whoever is doing this somehow knows of our connection, or at least sees us the same way. It's possible that Imka was murdered for her public positions on gene modification, but it could be she was killed by someone who knows about our society."

Callan's going to get us both killed!

Ansen took a deep breath. "With that as a consideration, I'm proposing that we consider inviting Madeline Blaze to join the Tree of Life Society with her contemporaries Adam Clayborn and Ensley Springer."

What? No! Ben Brown would roll over in his grave. He warned us these kinds of things would happen...and we responded too slow. I'll not make that mistake again.

The room grew quiet and then mumbling began. Zadie spoke above the side chatter. "I think it's something we should consider. And while we're at it, also consider her parents, Gwen and Ray."

The din grew with that suggestion until Master Fong entered the discussion. "I think we all know the dangers. Those women have a reputation for saying inflammatory things to grow their brand and sell music. One slip on a social media platform and our order collapses. What could possibly be worth that risk?"

Ansen drummed his fingers on the table once. "Put simply, our future. For six hundred years our society has worked toward a better world that is now attainable. These, and all other Tree of Life children will advance our entire species by never fearing, or falling prey to almost every known human illness. If we are to harness this advance, we must begin bringing members of that generation into our fellowship. As it turns out, Adam and Ensley have made this a condition of their joining."

Liza's hands balled into fists out of the camera's range. *What?*

The room was momentarily silent until Zadie filled the void. "Master Fong pointed out the risk, and I won't deny that possibility, but simply highlight the upside. Someone is trying to kill us, and now they've gone after a GM child. That WAGE group is trying to pass laws that make them second class citizens. We're fighting against that as hard as we can, but can you imagine the boost we could get if the most popular musician on the planet was coordinating with our messaging? That would be a huge force multiplier."

You traitor! I tried to kill you once, and as God is my witness, I'll keep trying until I do.

"On average we've brought in about one percent new outside membership each year." Ansen scanned the members around the table, as if gauging the reception of his argument. "It keeps our gene pool fresh and brings in powerful allies. I know it's a big risk, but as Zadie pointed out, it comes with major positive potential. I'm asking you to trust me in this first big decision as patriarch."

A hush fell over the room. "Are there any additional questions?" Ansen waited for a full silent ten-count. "Then we vote. All in favor raise your hand." Of the ten current members, eight quickly voted in favor.

Now eyes looked to both Master Fong and Liza. *I truly underestimated Ansen's political skills. I have to vote yes now or potentially raise suspicion.* She raised her hand and was quickly followed by Master Fong. *Just in time. It would have been just as bad to be last in a unanimous decision. I may have to play a more aggressive game if Ansen keeps this up.*

CHAPTER THIRTY-FIVE

Bree wrapped up a video meeting of climate advocates from around the world in preparation of the launch of the biggest carbon reduction plan in history. "What we do makes the world a better place for today's children as well as all future generations." With that, she clicked to end the virtual session. She mused. *Five years ago, I made the bargain to join the society partially in exchange for being able to lead this organization, and now look what we've accomplished. I hope the bargain we offer today has the same positive outcome, and doesn't blow up in our faces.*

It had been a week since the attack on Maddy and her recovery had been remarkable. It was both amazing and a little scary to see the real-life effects of the genetic alterations made to those fertilized eggs. None of them knew the full extent of their enhancements, but with Dr. Chavez coming to town in a couple of weeks, they hoped to get those answers, and more. But first it was time to change how Gwen, Ray and Maddy viewed the world. She glanced at her phone screen. *It's time.*

She exited her home office and began the long walk to the large covered patio. Along the way she strolled past the portraits of prior patriarchs that had been sent over from Prague. When she got to the end she stopped and gazed at the image of Kristoff and remembered the day he offered her society membership. After a few seconds her eyes moved to the empty space to the left. *Someday an artist will be commissioned to paint Ansen's portrait.*

When she stepped into the shaded outdoor space all interested parties were present. She joined Ansen at one end of a rectangular wrought iron table with glass top. Ray sat on a cushioned bench with Gwen while Maddy sipped lemonade with Ensley and Adam, all three with their feet propped up on the edges of the unlit firepit. Zadie and Kade had made the trip from Atlanta to add their perspective and support in what was sure to be a delicate discussion. "So good to see you all today, especially Maddy. You look great."

"Thanks, Mrs. Battle." She leaned forward and rubbed her lower leg that no longer showed any trace of the massive wound it had sustained. "Even my shattered tibia is completely healed."

Though that was an expected update, the news was still startling. "It was smart of you to call Adam and suggest he bring me to the hospital to get you out. I don't think the world is ready for this kind of news." Bree tentatively rubbed her hands together and began the discussion. "Which brings up why Ansen and I invited everyone here today."

Bree could both see and feel the stares from Maddy and her parents. *There's no normal way to do this, so here goes...* "Ray, Gwen, do you remember the day we met? The discussions we had?"

Ray's words sounded guarded. "Yes... It was when we all decided to go to the island in search of safety until these kids were born. What's that have to do with today?"

"Maddy was almost killed, and like when all of our lives were in danger then, we can offer protection."

"You mean like go to an island again? That's not going to work this time."

"We agree." She cut a quick glance at her husband, then continued easing toward the point of no return. "But we can lay out multiple options to keep all three of you safe... like everyone else here has already activated."

Gwen waved her arm in an arc. "You guys are in the fucking mob, right? I knew it five years ago."

God, I love your spirit... and I'm so sad this disease is killing you. "It's not the mob, it's something else, but here's the deal." Another swift look came Ansen's way. "You don't have to accept our help, but there's a catch. What we tell you next must never be told to anyone, ever. If revealed, people will die, likely including you three. It's your call if you want us to proceed."

Maddy popped up. "This is my life we're talking about, so I have a say in this, too." She turned to her friends. "You two know what she's talking about, right?"

They nodded in unison as Ensley reached for her hand. "It was actually our idea to tell you all, and we think you should listen to what they have to say."

She seemed to study her friends faces, then turned to her parents. "I trust these two with my life, so I vote to hear them out."

Ray put his arm around Gwen. "You live a transparent life, and I admire that so much. Are you willing to make and keep that promise to never tell anyone?"

Her reply was instant. "Maddy is my world and I would do anything to protect her. Go ahead, tell us this grand secret. I'll keep my mouth shut. I promise."

Bree took a cleansing breath and began. "There's no short version of what we're about to tell you, so just try to take it all in and save your questions until the end." With that Bree, Ansen, Zadie and Kade took turns telling the story of the Tree of Life Society. Bree wrapped it up. "So, not weird at all, right?"

Ray ran a hand through his hair. "I think I felt better when we thought you all were mafia. At least I could get my head around that." His cheeks puffed as he exhaled loudly. "But it sure explains a lot." He pointed. "Like the guard over there with the big gun."

Ensley had held Maddy's hand for the length of the telling of the story, and now spoke to her life-long friend. "We haven't kept this from you, Maddy. We just found out a few days ago and we insisted that you be included too, if that's what you choose."

With desperation in her voice, Gwen pleaded, her mood swings becoming more frequent. "And you can keep my Maddy safe?"

"I'm the patriarch, so I can offer the highest level of safety available in the world." His tone momentarily darkened. "We'll protect her as if she were our own, but you've seen first-hand the lengths to which our enemies will go."

Now a tear rolled down Gwen's face. "I won't be around much longer, so if you swear you'll watch over her, I'll join… and take the secret to my grave."

Ray held her close. "I'm not done fighting, so please don't give up." Suddenly his head snapped toward Ansen and Bree. "Chavez is still involved in all this, right?"

Ansen shrugged. "Yeah, she's the global medical director."

His eyes bulged as if they might come out of his head. "You're the boss. Would you direct her to turn the society's medical research toward finding a cure for Huntington's? Our children are living proof of what she can do, so it's possible that together, we can find the answer. You promise that, and I'm a yes as well."

Ansen's lips pulled tight, wanting nothing more than to fully grant his request. "I promise I will give her that directive, but you know her, I can't guarantee how she will respond."

Nodding vigorously, he agreed. "I know you'll do your best, and that means hope. I'm with Gwen, we're in."

In a blur, Maddy bolted to her parents in a tearful embrace. "I love you both so much! I'm in, too."

Ansen smiled. "Then we have a decision. I'll make the arrangements for a group initiation."

A happy mood consumed the space and group hugs abounded. A memory flashed in Bree's mind of when she faced her brain cancer life or death decision. Miguel's words rang as true today as when he said them to her five years ago. *When the decision is between living or dying, it's always simple.*

CHAPTER THIRTY-SIX

A festive mood filled every corner of Becky and Kelley's small apartment. Every corner except the one where Becky had seated herself. She had only agreed to host the event at Kelley's persistent urging, being told it would lift her mood, but it was having the opposite effect. She was already working on her fourth whisky sour, somewhat masking her true feelings. *I'll be glad when all these people leave.*

Phillip strolled up with a smile as broad as the Brooklyn Bridge. "It's been too long, sister, I haven't seen you since the night your nose was broken. I'm thinking it's about time for a little payback."

She was about to answer when the first cords of the Madeline Blaze song, *You See Me, I See You,* played over the speakers, spinning Becky up in a frenzy. "Turn that bitch's song off!" Her outburst momentarily silenced the room, and with a big gulp she finished off her drink. As the noise slowly returned and a new song began, she snarled at Phillip. "I'm heading to the bar."

Kelley, dressed in a stylish emerald green maternity dress, was chatting with Agnes and Ian as Becky walked by, stumbling and nearly falling before catching her balance. Kelley quickly came to her side. "You okay, dear?"

Trying to contain her emotions in front of her wife had taken an additional toll on her disposition, but she continued to bite her tongue. "No worries, Sweetie. Just tripped on the rug, that's all."

"Maybe that's a sign to have a club soda instead, like me." Kelley cradled Becky's hand, then kissed her cheek. "It's only ten o'clock."

It took all the willpower she could muster to contain her feeling of undirected rage. She answered through a forced smile. "I'll think about it." She gently pulled her hand away and took the last few steps toward the collection of various alcoholic beverages on the small kitchen island. *There, I've thought about it, and decided another whisky sour is exactly what I need. In fact, I'll make it a double.*

Phillip caught up as she was stirring lemon juice, simple sugar and whiskey with a swizzle stick in a chunky tumbler. "Hey, we okay? Did I say something that pissed you off?"

Sampling the drink, she decided that a double was definitely the right choice. "It's not you, it's me." That statement was where the full truth telling ended. "It's just that with Kelley expecting, it's not a good time to risk anything, as much as I want to take another run at them." It was what he needed to hear, but it wasn't the whole story. On the mission targeting Madeline Blaze, she had fired the shot that killed one of the eight people that died that day, and her conscience was wrestling with her rage. Neither part of her brain able to overcome the other, leaving her miserable.

Mixing a rum and coke, he nodded. "I get it, that's the mature thing to do. But I know how this must be eating at you, so I've come up with an idea. I'll get the rest of the RAGE gang together and we'll bust a few heads and record it for you. It won't be the same, but it will be something."

An image of what that would be like briefly flashed in her mind, triggering a smile, before being replaced by one of him being executed by a society team for breaking the deal she made with that trio. *And what was I thinking going on that raid with Callan? If I were found out, then Kelley, myself and our baby would be dead. Moron!* She took another drink and kept lying. "I know you would do anything for me, and I appreciate it. But promise me you won't, because I want revenge to come from my own hand. Don't worry, when I do it, you'll be right there beside me."

Elbowing her, he changed the subject. "Somebody almost beat you to it. What did you think of that attack on that Blaze girl? I'll give'm props, those people had balls attacking her in broad daylight."

Regret about her role in the murder of eight people had touched every waking moment, and most of her dreams since. The words tumbled out drenched in cynicism. "Yeah. I'll say."

He grabbed her by the arm with his free hand. "What's wrong with you? We hate those people and someone almost did us a huge favor! Am I missing something?"

Her first response was a forearm shove. "Grab me like that again, and you'll be the one almost dead."

Both hands went up in mock surrender as the right hand tried not to spill his rum and coke. "Jeez, Becky! Chill. We're on the same team, or at least I thought we were."

Her shoulders fell as she tried to right the situation. "Sorry, man. I've just had a lot on my mind, you know, with the baby and all." *Time to shut this convo down.* She leaned closer and whispered. "And it's that time of the month, if you know what I mean." *That always works with guys.*

"Oh - we're cool. It's all good." He backed up and glanced at her now empty tumbler. "Can I make you another?"

She looked at the glass she had just drained and tilted her head, the alcohol finally numbing her raging brain enough to cope with all the people in her space. "Yeah. They seem to be going down easy tonight."

CHAPTER THIRTY-SEVEN

Despite all that had gone on lately, Adam practically skipped into Chalky's. He had just finished shooting a television segment to be aired on a Sunday news show highlighting his bank's dramatic growth that at the same time was helping tens of thousands of small entrepreneurs in some of the poorest places on earth. Combined with his and Ensley's success in getting Maddy and her parents into the society, he felt like he was on a massive winning streak. Even though two body guards now accompanied him wherever he went, his words radiated energy as he walked into the lively scene. "Hey Kimee, looks like it's shaping up as another epic Saturday night."

Her one-word reply rang flat. "Sure." Then she turned and began the familiar walk to the VIP section. "Expecting company tonight?" She asked, diverting her glance.

"Yeah, Ensley said she would stop by." He touched her arm. "You okay? I'm used to the perky Kimee."

Her gaze now met his in a look he couldn't quite identify. "Just a lot going on right now." Once again, she looked away. "I'll let Chalky know you're here."

He followed. *Wonder what's up with her?* That thought evaporated as he saw Ens enter with her own detail of armed protectors. She wore a shimmering ombre sequined mini-dress that seemed to reflect every light in the humming club. *Damn, that's a statement without saying a word.*

Kimee delivered Ens to the table, who immediately gave Adam a tight embrace. She whispered. "So good to see you tonight."

Her greeting boosted his already good mood. *Could tonight get any better?*

"Chalky said he would be up in a bit." While not as off as earlier, the hostess still didn't seem her normal self. "We're featuring mojitos tonight, would you like to start with one of those, or something else?"

Ens gave a shoulder shrug, then glanced at Adam, who nodded. "Sounds good, Kimee. Thanks."

After she was out of earshot, Adam asked Ens, "does she seem different to you tonight?"

Glancing over her shoulder, Ens replied. "I didn't notice anything." She turned back toward Adam. "I've been looking forward to tonight all week. It seems like I've been under house arrest with these guards around all the time, and I'm tired of working twelve-hours a day from home. It's time to live a little."

His eyes darted for a second to her shapely figure sparkling in the multicolored lights. "I couldn't agree more."

Chalky made his way to the table. "Welcome! Always glad to have two of my favorite people in the house." He glanced at the muscular guards who accompanied Adam and Ensley. "Sign of the times?"

Ens answered first. "You know it. After what happened here, and then with Maddy, they go where we go. At least we can afford it, I feel sorry for the so many who might also be targeted and can't."

"I get that. Speaking of Maddy, how is she?"

Adam's half smile hid the full truth. His practiced white lie sounded convincing. "Her injuries weren't as bad as first reported. In fact, she thought about joining us here tonight."

Chalky shook his head. "I still can't believe that happened, it's a dangerous world. Speaking of dangerous, I saw that woman, Becky Brown, on TV today. She said she thinks her WAGE group has enough votes to get that anti-genetic-modification bill through congress."

Just the mention of that name caused Adam's face to harden. "All she does is trade in hate. I have a feeling she'll get what she deserves someday."

Kimee reappeared with the first round of drinks for the table, set them down in silence, then walked away. Adam asked. "What's up with Kimee? She's usually all bubbly and weird…in a good way."

Chalky's head tilted. "I don't know for sure, said she's got some decisions to make. I try to stay out of my employee's personal lives."

Ensley raised her glass. "Enough serious talk, we're here to have a good time. Yori is the DJ and the company is fine. Let's make it a night to remember."

In a microsecond glance, Adam again checked out Ensley's figure. *A night to remember. I totally agree.* Their glasses clinked and *Freak Flag* began playing loudly. "I think that's our sign to hit the floor."

As the night wore on, the crowd continued to get larger pushing the grooving bodies closer. Five drinks and two hours of dancing later, Adam had his courage up, overcoming self-doubt about whether what he was about to say was a good idea. With just the slightest quiver in his voice he said what he had wanted to for a long time. "Hey, Ens. What do you think about taking the party back to my place?"

Her arms were around his neck as they moved in unison to the music. After making him wait a few seconds she stopped dancing and stood on her tiptoes to kiss his cheek before leaning closer, answering in a sexy whisper. "What took you so long to ask?"

When the song ended, they waved goodbye to both Chalky and Yori before heading toward the exit, with four large men surrounding them. Reaching the door, Adam caught a glimpse of Kimee, who stood statue still, with a vacant brooding stare. He was about to go over, but Ens tugged his arm letting him know the car had been brought around.

"Are you ready?"

Seeing the dimples in her cheeks and hearing the sweet notes of her words, he turned away from Kimee, his thoughts completely diverted. He reached for her hand and squeezed. "Like never before."

CHAPTER THIRTY-EIGHT

Phillip and Anfernee waited in the darkened van in the parking lot near Chalky's, watching the last few partiers straggle out. Phillip glanced at his phone, then snorted a white line of coke on a shiny black piece of acrylic he kept in the glovebox for just such an occasion. "Four-thirty. He should be coming out soon."

Anfernee pointed to the tricked out red Lexus RC sports coupe. "You sure that's his car?"

He felt his buzz intensify. "Positive. He finds a way to include it in one of his Instagram posts at least once a week. Japanese guy, Japanese car." Phillip reached toward the digital camera temporarily mounted to the dash. "This should get great footage for Becky and Kelley. I don't care what Becky says, she'll love it."

"Yeah... oh, look. There he is." Anfernee made a head motion toward the gate. "The one and only Yori Kobayashi. You ready to do this?"

Phillip patted the matte-gray Glock 19 resting on his leg, then started the recording. "Absolutely. He comes with us willingly, or we rough him up here. We can't just stand by while they take over the world." As Yori got closer, his right hand grasped the molded grip. "Let's do this. We go on three. One-Two-Three!"

Simultaneously they jumped out of the van and quickly covered the short distance between them and their target, the weapon now raised to firing position. "Hands up and nobody gets hurt!"

Yori froze. "I don't want any trouble." He half raised his hands. "Take my money... my phone." He motioned toward his car. "Take my ride, too. It's worth a lot."

A laughing Phillip was playing to the camera. "We don't want your stinking car, Jap boy, we're here for you."

Taking a step back, Yori pleaded. "No, guys. I'm sure we can work something out. Let's just talk about this."

Phillip's tone turned menacing. "Do what you're told and you might live. Make this hard for us and you die here. You understand...freak!" He waved the gun, "now get on the ground."

Yori went down on one knee. "Hey, boss. Nobody's done anything they'll regret yet. Please, take my stuff and call it a win. Please?"

"Tie his hands, Anfernee. We need to get out of here."

Moving closer, Anfernee reached for Yori's right hand, but it moved in a blur just before his grasp closed. A second later Yori was standing and delivering a blow to his aggressor's neck. A snapping noise was followed by an 'oof' sound as Anfernee's limp body fell to the pavement.

Yori began backing away as Phillip yelled, his arrogance replaced by terror. "Anfernee!! Anfernee! Get up man, quit messing around!"

Taking another step, Yori spoke calmly. "Check on your friend. He needs you."

Phillip rushed to Anfernee's side and saw unblinking, unfocused eyes reflecting the parking lot florescent lighting, and he knew what that meant. His rage exploded as he raised the weapon, looking for Yori, who was now running away. "You're a dead man!"

The first bullet found its mark, dropping Yori in a heap. He flailed, trying to get back up, but faltering. Phillip was on him in seconds. "You FREAK!! He was my best friend!"

"I'm…"

Boom, Boom. Two bullets to the back of Yori's skull ended the conversation. Standing between two dead bodies, his rage morphed into fear and his hands shook as he held the gun. "How…"

No more words would form as he spun in the direction of his friend. Seeing his body, he froze for a moment, then willed his legs to run back to Anfernee. Kneeling beside him and checking for a pulse he knew wasn't there, convulsive sobs wracked his body. "We were just going to have some fun and rough him up. No!"

The sound of sirens interrupted his grieving as he rubbed his friend's shoulder. "I'm so sorry. This wasn't supposed to happen." The evolutionary fight or flight response kicked in, momentarily overriding all other emotions. He grabbed the gun and dragged Anfernee's limp body back to the van, wrestling it through the side door, then made a fast exit from the scene. Light rain began to fall as he made his way out of the city. Thoughts escaped his lips in a whisper. "What have I done?" He drove on. "And what do I do now?"

CHAPTER THIRTY-NINE

Ansen and Bree waited in his home office for Dr. Chavez to arrive. A few weeks had passed since she had hinted at a secret they needed to know. When the doorbell rang, he sighed, then looked toward his wife. "Even after knowing her for five years, I'm still nervous around her."

Standing, Bree gave a slight shoulder shake. "Yeah, totally."

Seeing her walk in, Ansen had the distinct impression that she acted more as if he were visiting her office than the other way around. Her words matched that assessment. "Please, sit."

He sat behind his own desk hoping to project at least a little authority. "Thank you for coming, you're always welcome in our home."

Her eyes wandered around the spacious room. "I approve. This is a place worthy of housing the patriarch."

Since when do I need your approval... forget it. Our business is too important to get hung up on her power trip. "We're settling in."

"Congratulations on your election." Her chin lowered as she stared over her black-framed glasses. "In time, I'm sure you'll grow into the role."

Gritting his teeth under a thin tight smile, he kept his temper in check. "I appreciate your vote of confidence." His hand flexed as he continued. "We've invited you here to talk about two important things. First, Gwen Blaze, her husband, and their daughter have been invited to join the society, and they've accepted... on a condition that involves you."

Raising her eyebrows, she commented. "So, the band from the Caribbean island will finally all sing from the same hymnal. Interesting. And the other topic?"

Ansen delivered a furtive glance toward his wife. "The other reason is that a few weeks ago you mentioned that there was information we need to know, and would likely only find out if I were chosen as the patriarch." He took a breath. "It's time for us to learn that secret."

"Hmmm. Let's first address the musical family who could sing to the world and ruin everything. What could they possibly want from me?"

"Their whole reason for going the GM route with Madeline was to spare her from the disease that haunts their family." Ansen leaned in. "Unfortunately, that specter has its grips on Gwen. She's exhibiting the signs, and they appear to be aggressive."

The doctor's expression didn't change. "That is regrettable, but not unexpected. What does that have to do with me?"

Bree joined in the conversation. "As you know, we're in a global fight for all of our children against these laws from that WAGE group. Gwen and Maddy have agreed to ramp up their considerable influence around the world against those people, if you agree to join them in research to stop Huntington's Disease. We could use their help."

For the first time today, the start of a smile on her bright red lips emerged. "I've underestimated those two yet again. They had a little leverage and used it. Bravo for them."

Bree continued pressing the case, just as she and Ansen had discussed. "It would be a blessing to the world if you could do for Huntington's, what you did in finding the cure for the brain cancer I had." She readied to pitch their strongest argument. "And a second Nobel Prize in medicine would look good on your mantel."

The smile grew by a few millimeters. "It would gall the hell out of that Stockholm crowd if they had to give me another one, wouldn't it?"

"And put you in a class by yourself as the greatest scientist... ever."

Ansen smiled inside, admiring how well Bree had played their cards. "What do you say? Think you can do it?"

They sat quietly, waiting for an answer, finally seeing a full smile. "I'll call Miguel and have him start making arrangements."

A sigh of relief preceded Ansen's reply. "You've made our day. Gwen and her family thank you, and so do we."

While happy the doctor was onboard to help Gwen and Ray, he remained on edge because he knew there was more to learn concerning Adam. He guided the conversation. "Because of your cryptic advice, I placed my name in contention for this role. I have to tell you, I've been more than a little anxious about what we're about to hear."

Her all business demeanor returned in microseconds. "Yes. It's a conversation we need to have, but must stay between us until the time is right. Will you swear to tell no one?"

Those words chilled him, because having seen her up close for the past few years, he understood that when she swore someone to secrecy, it was important and probably dangerous. He looked at Bree knowing they had no choice but to agree to her terms. "We swear."

Folding her hands, the doctor began. "For the past six centuries, the goal of the society has been to provide a better life for our children. We've done that incrementally over the years, and starting with your son, the progress has been in leaps and bounds." She glanced around the room. "Do you have a bar in here? I want a drink, and you might need one as well."

Ansen walked to a closed cabinet, opened it and pulled out a bottle of Blanton's bourbon and three tumblers. "I'm still getting settled, so this is what I have."

The doctor nodded. "Perfect... and make mine a double."

Ansen made the pours, then took a seat beside Bree. "We're as ready as we'll ever be."

Raising her glass, Chavez gulped half. "A few weeks ago, you saw the most dramatic evidence yet of the self-healing properties engineered into his DNA." She paused and took another sip. "Well, that's only the beginning."

Bree nodded. "When we saw that, we assumed as much, and we now know that Ensley and Madeline have similar abilities. What else should we expect?"

She laughed. "I see I've underestimated Ray yet again. I wasn't sure he had the skill to make those edits in that embryo. No one else in the world can." Then her mood changed on a dime as she pointed her finger, eyes moving between them. "Swear to me that you won't tell those children or their parents until they're ready, it could ruin everything if they learn too soon. Promise?"

Their hands grasped tight as they answered. "We promise."

She finished her drink and cradled the empty tumbler in her hands. "Because of this healing capacity, they will have a very long life with cells regenerating perfectly, aging very slowly. If you think about it, that will be both a blessing and a curse."

Bree's words trembled. "For how long?"

Dr. Chavez gazed past them into some seeming distant view. "A very long time." Sitting still, her eyes widened without blinking. "This is the truth you must protect. What was once only a dream is now reality. Those three might live forever, and with their healing abilities, they are nearly immortal."

CHAPTER FORTY

As was his custom, Adam woke early and like a couple of weeks ago, he was both excited and nervous seeing a woman sleeping in bed beside him. While the experiences were similar, there were clearly differences. He had been nervous with Kimee because he barely knew her. It was the exact opposite with Ensley. In fact, he couldn't remember not knowing her, and before puberty kicked in, thought of her as a sister. After last night, he knew he would never see her that way again.

As if her body was synced with his, she rolled over. "Hey."

"Hey there yourself."

She giggled, then snuggled beside him, her words soft as she touched his face. "Just so you know, I had a good time."

He knew his smile was a mile wide. "I think you know I did."

With her delicate fingers resting on his chest, a question came, framed in an uncertain voice. "What's next?"

Adam gazed into her nearly black eyes fully aware that he probably looked like a happy puppy. "I have no idea, and for some reason, I don't care. The here and now is good enough for me."

The return smile was so large it caused her eyes to squint. "I like it to... but we have that initiation ceremony this afternoon and we need to decide how public or private we want this..." she paused as if searching for the right descriptor and failing, "this whatever it is, to be. Any suggestions?"

"I'm sure I don't want to tell anyone today. My parents will be wound tighter than a Spanx girdle."

A laugh was her initial response. "Mine too." She was quiet for a moment. "Any idea what you want, you know, down the road."

"I would be proud to be your special someone, but let's take our time and be smart. We both have high profile careers, so let's only tell the rest of the world when we're ready. Deal?"

"Deal." Her index finger touched his chin. "I know a great way to start the day, if you're interested."

The suggestive words were like a shot of adrenaline, heightening all his senses to their highest level. Then her hand slid over his waist, pulling them closer. His answer was certain. "I'm definitely interested."

The morning of sensuality that followed somehow topped last night's all-time high, finishing with laying in each other's arms looking up at the ceiling. A single word escaped his lips. "Wow."

She reached for his hand. "I'll say. Sunday morning the way it should be."

His mind replayed their morning in exquisite detail as they shared a few minutes of silence. He rolled up on an elbow, admiring her toned body. "I'm starved. How about a shower, then grab a bite of breakfast?"

Giggling exactly like earlier in the morning, she asked, "is your shower big enough for two?"

He couldn't get the word 'yes' out fast enough.

After their sudsy encounter, Ens was in agreement with Adam. "I'm starved, too. Know anyplace close?"

"Actually, I do. It's just around the corner."

Soon, they were devouring lox and bagels, washing it down with strong coffee. Ens reached across the table, placing her hand over his. "Last night...this morning. It still doesn't feel real. It's like it was some kind of wonderful dream and I'm afraid I'll wake up and it will be gone."

He turned his hand over, palm up, to hold hers. "It's just the opposite for me. It's the most real thing I've ever experienced. I've never felt surer of something... or more alive." Leaning close, he gently kissed her inviting lips until being interrupted by the ringing of his phone. "It's Chalky. Wonder what's up with him?"

As Adam took the call, Ens pulled out her phone to scroll through Instagram posts seeing what was going on in the rest of the world. Her eyes opened wider as she scrolled, seeming not to hear Adam's voice.

"Ens! Ens! Look at me!" He saw a face registering shock when she looked up. "What's wrong?"

A shaky reply returned. "You go first. What's with Chalky?"

His tongue felt dry, as if his mouth was full of cotton balls, and he spoke slowly. "It's Yori... he's dead."

"No! That can't be, we just saw him last night!"

Adam's entire body went numb as he explained. "He was murdered in the parking lot after the club closed. That's all Chalky knows."

Both hands went behind her head, fingers interlacing. "No, it can't be!" Her eyes widened. "I bet it was those WAGE thugs."

He nodded. "I guess our warning wasn't strong enough." The muscles in his jaw rippled as he gritted his teeth. "They'll pay for this."

"I agree, but we have another problem to deal with first."

"What?" His forehead creased. "What are you talking about?"

She handed him her phone and he saw a photo taken anonymously just moments ago, of he and Ensley kissing, and already spreading around the world at the speed of light. "So much for the plan of letting the world know when we're ready. It really is going to be a day we'll never forget."

CHAPTER FORTY-ONE

Her ringing phone jolted Liza from her early Sunday morning sleep, and the name that appeared on the screen was unexpected. "Becky?"

Becky's trembling voice set Liza on edge. "Sorry to bug you so early, but I don't know who else to call."

Sitting upright, the sheet and duvet were pushed back. "What's wrong?"

"Two of my friends did something stupid last night and they need help... special help."

The terrified tone told Liza as much as Becky's words. "Don't say anything else, okay? I'll meet you in an hour in Central Park. I'll be on a bench near Bethesda Terrace."

"I know the place. Thank you."

Liza wanted to say, *don't thank me yet*, but instead reassured the younger woman. "I've got your back."

The call ended and Liza set about getting dressed, mumbling as she buttoned her navy, silk blouse. "This better not blow back on me." In short order she was sitting on a bench watching joggers log miles on a sunny day, finally spying Beck walking past flowering plants toward her. Liza raised the spare cup she had purchased. "I brought you a coffee. I hope one cream and two sugars works."

"Thanks, sounds like exactly what I need." She sat down beside Liza and her shoulders sagged.

Seeing Becky's splotchy face, Liza knew her news was bad.

"What did your friends do to upset you?"

Becky's lips pulled tight. "I warned them. I said chill for now on harassing freaks... but they didn't listen... and now a freak is dead... and so is one of my friends."

Liza's muscles tensed and her voice lowered. "Is it one of those first three?"

"No, but it's one of their friends." Becky leaned her head back and dug the heels of her palms into her closed eyes. "Why didn't they listen?"

Hearing that it wasn't one of those three, Liza's demeanor warmed a degree as she remembered Becky's father, Ben. He hadn't listened to her warnings, and it cost him his life. "As much as we might love them, sometimes they're just too hard-headed to hear us." She reached for Becky's hand. "What kind of help do you need?"

She told Liza the story of how Yori Kobayashi killed Anfernee, and in turn was murdered by Phillip. "He's driving around the backroads of New Jersey with his best friend's body in the back of the van, and no clue what to do next. Neither do I, so I called you."

She wanted to scream. *Those idiots are going to get us all killed.* But instead, she decided the best course was take to care of the mess, fast. "I'll make a call to Callan. He'll know how to dispose of the body and get your friend away from here. He'll have to go far away for a long time and maybe even need a new identity."

Becky's clasped hands rested in her lap and her thumbs fidgeted. "Anfernee and Phillip sure screwed us! Adam Clayborn had people a lot like Callan working for him, and his warning to us was crystal clear. What should Kelley and I do now?"

Liza knew that Becky and Kelley had a run-in with the three, but was shocked to learn this detail about the firepower they had at their disposal. "Really?" She pondered for a moment. "That certainly raises the threat level." Her brain spooled through options, until arriving at an answer. "Call Kelley and have her get bags packed. There's a safe house, a cabin in the woods actually. We used it in the old days and I kept it off the books. It's basic, but very secluded, and that's what we need right now."

Striking her own forehead with an open palm, Becky vented. "Fuck, fuck, fuck! Kelley's going to hate this. In fact, she might kill me even if those freaks don't."

Liza stood and offered her hand, helping Becky stand. "Do what I say and we'll all get through this." She hugged the young woman as another thought ran through her mind. *And if this turns on me, I'll kill you myself, if that's what it takes for me to survive.*

CHAPTER FORTY-TWO

Adam and Ensley walked into his parent's new country home together, unsure of what kind of reception they would receive knowing that the anonymous kissing photo had spread widely. Adam whispered to her as they were about to enter the den. "Guess we'll find out how plugged in our parents are."

His mother's welcome gave him his answer. "Anything you two want to announce?"

Looking around the room, it was if they were facing a jury of Maddy and her parents, as well as Dr. Chavez and both sets of their parents. Adam felt his cheeks warming. "I guess everyone's seen the picture?"

They all nodded as Zadie spoke, appearing to direct the comment toward her daughter. "Well?"

Ensley reached for Adam's hand and shrugged. "I don't know what you want us to say, because we don't even know what to call it. Whatever it is, it's new. Less than twenty-four hours old."

Ansen finally ended an awkward silence. "Then we'll tend to other business." He pointed to an open loveseat. "We've received information on the murder of your friend."

A bitter taste filled Adam's mouth as he sat, still holding Ensley's hand. "What do you know?"

Glancing at Ray and Gwen, Ansen began. "As those about to join our order will soon learn, we have vast resources at our disposal, including in most major police departments. While this evil act didn't affect a society member, we take keen interest in all violence against the growing GM population."

Maddy interrupted. "It was Becky Brown and those WAGE people, wasn't it?"

Ansen's head tilted slightly. "You're half right. Although the surveillance camera at the parking lot had been disabled by the perps, there was another across the street they missed. The police got a clear look at the license plate on a van belonging to one Phillip Poppins. Police assume he was one of the two men involved in the attack."

Adam felt his anger growing. "We know he's one of them. If we track him down, I'm sure he can be persuaded to ID his friend."

"That won't be necessary. Yori put up a fight and apparently killed the second man, before being shot himself."

For several seconds no one said a word, each seeming to process the information until Ensley spoke. "What do we do now?"

Ansen pointed to each of the young people. "You three don't do anything. The society has been handling situations like this for centuries and we'll take it from here. Are we clear?"

Weak "yeses" were mumbled back.

Ansen clapped his hands once. "Alright then, let's put this tragic business aside for a while and turn our attention to the joyful reason we're all gathered." His tone brightened. "It's initiation day for five of you, a day you will remember for the rest of your lives. Bree and I will help you find the bedrooms where you'll be changing, and after the ceremony, we'll celebrate."

As everyone stood and began milling around, Maddy approached Adam and Ens, hands in her jeans pockets and speaking as if she were searching for the right words. "So, guys...what the hell?"

Ensley touched her shoulder. "We're so sorry, we certainly didn't want you to find out this way."

Her right hand came out of her pocket and gripped the back of her neck. "Forget how I found out, I'm just totally blindsided. I don't even know what to say."

Now it was Adam who put his hands in his pockets. "I don't either, but what I do know is there is no one else like us in the world. No matter what happens with Ens and I, the three of us have to stick together. Agreed?"

Ensley pulled him closer and his hands wrapped around the two women in a group hug. She squeezed them both. "Together for life."

As Adam repeated those words with one arm holding each woman, try as he might, he couldn't stop his brain from wondering. *Did I make the right choice?*

CHAPTER FORTY-THREE

Liza had made up an excuse to stay in New York longer instead of returning home to Atlanta. Too much was going on with Becky and Kelley and the efforts to hide Phillip. Because of her proximity, she had been invited to join Ansen at his home for a video meeting with the council. After a tour of the place, she sat by his side awaiting the start of the call. As he stared at his computer, she made a mental note. *I liked Kristoff's place better, but I could certainly upgrade to a place like this when I take over... and my time WILL come. Just because he's the sperm donor for the first GM freak, he feels entitled. I mean, he's only been on the council five years while I've invested a lifetime!*

At the appointed time, the screen began to fill with the faces of the other members joining from their homes. Ansen kicked off the call. "Good afternoon everyone, welcome. I have three agenda items, then we'll cover regular business."

Good. Short and sweet so I can get as far from this man as possible.

He continued. "First up is to report that all three of our first special children, as well as Gwen Blaze and her husband, are now official Tree of Life Society members."

Liza kept a straight face as she thought. *How different my life would be if we had killed them all five years ago.*

Charlotte chimed in from Sydney. "That had to have been the strangest initiation ever. How did it go?"

Ansen laughed lightly as his chin lifted. "I'll never forget it. Seeing them all in their black robes at the beginning of the ceremony, I felt like a high school principle on graduation day. It was the first one I've officiated as the patriarch and our first three special children, including my son, are now members. I was very proud."

His tone darkened and Ansen's words now sounded more somber. "On a serious note, it was tough to see Gwen Blaze struggling to remember even the few lines she was asked to recite. Her disease seems to be advancing rapidly."

Master Fong intoned. "That is very sad. With Dr. Chavez involved there must be hope for the family."

Ansen's eyebrows raised. "Yes, that's true. But if you could have seen her, you would know that it would take a miracle."

Now Sameer spoke from Seattle. "And that hope will keep them quiet. I still worry she could ruin everything by exposing us."

She could see that Sameer's comment bothered Ansen, but after a hard stare at the screen, he moved on. "That brings me to our second item." He paused, his words taking an even darker tone. "As some of you may have seen on the news, a GM person was murdered here in the city a few days ago. While he wasn't a society member, we take all violence against modified people seriously, and this case does have links to us. He was close friends with our first three."

Damn it. I was afraid something like this would happen. She hung on every word as Ansen continued.

"But there's something even more concerning. The two perpetrators have a connection to the old reformers."

Mumbles poured in from around the entire globe until Sameer spoke loudly. "I knew something was off when Imka was killed, I knew it in my gut. Has a faction of those people taken up the battle again?"

Lisa subtly glanced at Sameer's square on the screen. *Those people? You voted for me, but I guess I know what you really think of me now. Maybe you'll be next on my list instead of Zadie.*

Ansen's lips pursed. "We're still putting the pieces together. What we do know is that the two men who were involved in this murder are known associates of Becky Brown and Kelley Slaughter." He paused, as if for effect. "I think everyone recognizes those surnames."

Becky's friend assured her he had gotten away unseen. This is the worst-case scenario.

Charlotte asked. "So, what's your plan?"

He stared into the camera. "On the plus side, this does help ensure that neither Blaze woman will be tempted to spill anything about us as we are providing protection to them all. They know that Madeline could be targeted again, and our protection can keep her safe. They would never jeopardize her safety."

A voice of approval came from Australia. "An unexpected plus. What else?"

His voice lowered. "One of the attackers was also killed in the assault, so the main focus is tracking down the surviving murderer. At the same time, we're searching for Becky Brown and Kelley Slaughter. They seem to have gone underground, but we've got some leads. When we find them, we need to have a Tree of Life Society chat with all three."

I was wrong, THIS is the worst-case scenario.

Master Fong rejoined the conversation. "Agreed. We need to end this threat before it grows. You said three agenda items today, Ansen. What is the third?"

"Thanks for the segue." Ansen's delivery remained serious. "I know the tragic loss of Imka remains fresh in our minds, but as a council, we need to move forward with replacements. Combined with Kristoff's passing and my ascension, we have two open seats."

Hmm. This should be interesting.

Briefly bowing, Master Fong continued. "I still grieve their loss." His serene dark eyes stared on their screen. "Have we made any progress in identifying Imka's killer?"

Ansen's quick nod put Liza on edge, waiting on his reply. *What do they know?*

"I'm proud to say, yes. We got a tip from a source in the Newark police department. There was a bar fight and two men were arrested. Nothing notable in that, but he recognized the man who bailed them out. He's known to us."

Liza could feel dread shooting up her spine like an icy spike. *Please, no. Don't say his name.*

The next words from Ansen's mouth confirmed her fearful premonition. "Callan McDougal is in town, and I don't think it's a coincidence."

Zadie's response was instant. "He's the one who tried to kill us!" Her face looked pale on the screen, but her words blazed hot. "It's time for payback. Tell me we have a location and I'll join the team that goes after him."

Ansen held his hand up. "I share your desire for revenge, but we haven't tracked him down yet. Hopefully we'll locate his hideout in the coming days, and finally rid this world of a killer and an enemy."

Stay calm, just be cool until this meeting is over. It's time to rethink everything.

While her voice wasn't as loud, Liza still felt Zadie's rage as she repeated her offer. "Remember, I'm available to join that team on a moment's notice."

A slight head bob acknowledged the comment, then Ansen continued. "Message received." He paused for a moment before directing the call back to a replacement member. "As we were discussing, it's time for us to once again replenish our council."

To keep appearances normal, Liza asked the obvious question. "Who do you have in mind?"

His shoulders tensed as he answered. "I have an idea for one of the openings now, but I'm not sure if she would accept. I can't think of anyone who has been more important to our order in the past few years." He drew in a breath. "With your approval, I submit that Dr. Cielo Chavez should join our council."

Chavez?

No one made a sound or said a word as Ansen waited for their reaction. "Well?" He asked after several long seconds.

Ever the diplomat, Master Fong offered the first feedback. "No one can match her contributions, or question her credentials." He folded his hands in front of himself. "That said, she has never been what one would call a team player."

The tilt of his head and raised eyebrows signaled everyone. "I know that better than most, believe me, but she has a brilliant mind and never hesitates when a big decision needs to be made. If anyone else has someone better qualified, now is the time to speak, otherwise I'll assume your support."

No other names were offered as Ansen waited a full fifteen seconds. "Then I'll make the call. It is entirely possible that she will decline the invitation, because as Master Fong said, she likes to fly solo. I thank everyone for your backing of my decision."

The topics pivoted to mundane subjects as Liza listened, sitting as still as a statue while her muscles itched to take her away from this situation. Soon the meeting adjourned and she said her goodbyes, leaving as soon as possible, anxious to put plans in place to save herself. She mulled her options as the chauffeur drove her back to the city with an armed escort following. *First, I talk with Callan. We have much to discuss and so many loose ends to tie up before one of them gets us both killed. Phillip Poppins knows way too much... so he must be dealt with. And Callan's two sloppy men? I know how that will play out.*

Then her mind turned to the toughest decision. *What to do about Becky and Kelley? I don't want to kill them, but if it's them or me...* A smirk crawled across her face. *Chavez isn't the only one who never hesitates to act.*

CHAPTER FORTY-FOUR

After days of working from his parent's secure home, Adam was dying to get out of the house, and Chalky's birthday celebration was just the excuse he needed. His mother had protested, but he reassured her. "Mom, all three of us will have armed bodyguards. We'll be safe, I promise."

She didn't seem pleased. "Your friend was killed at that place." Her fingers rubbed her temple. "I know you're full grown, but sometimes I only see a five-year-old when I look at you, and I worry."

Adam put his arm around her shoulder. "Come on, mom. I usually act at least eighteen."

She elbowed him. "You better, or I'll ground you." After more teasing he headed for the back door as she gave one last bit of advice. "Be careful."

"Always."

As he rode in the back seat of the black SUV he thought about Ensley and how they hadn't been together since that first night. He texted his mother. *Don't wait up, I may stay at my place tonight.*

His phone dinged with a quick reply. *Damn it, Adam. This is serious.*

I'll be careful, I promise. There will be enough guards there to make a complete basketball team with a substitute player.

He laughed upon receiving a string of emojis indicating her frustration. After the hour-long drive, he bounced into the club as the first of the trio to arrive.

Kimee greeted him with what sounded like a twist of sarcasm. "Here alone, or will your girlfriend be joining?"

He answered defensively. "Actually, the three of us. Some things might have changed, but we'll always be friends."

"Hmm, interesting. Follow me and I'll let Chalky know you're here."

Watching her walk, the old exaggerated swish was still missing. When they got to the table, he touched her arm. "You okay?"

Glancing away, she mumbled. "Yeah... I'm alright... I guess. Got some things on my mind."

Adam pulled out a chair. "Please, sit and talk. Sometimes it's good just to let it out and maybe get a fresh perspective."

Shaking her head, she demurred, sounding as if she might cry. "No, not here. Not tonight."

Although it had just been a one-night stand, he genuinely felt they shared a kindred spirit, and he clearly had resources to help out in most situations. "Hey, I'm your friend. Let me help."

Turning toward him, he saw glistening eyes and raised shoulders. "Maybe we could meet for lunch?"

Hearing the offer, he felt good. "Deal. I'll text tomorrow and we'll meet."

Her cheeks lifted as she answered in a voice barely loud enough to hear above the noise of the partiers. "Thanks. Sounds like a plan."

She walked away with a little more pep. *She's a nice girl, I hope I can help.* His thoughts turned quickly as he saw Maddy enter with her own set of bodyguards. *Now, let's see how this goes. Mine and Ensley's relationship outing seemed to rattle her.*

Maddy's stroll to the VIP section was slower than his, as adoring fans pleaded for selfies with the singer. She indulged more times than not. Her mood seemed relaxed as she joined Adam. "It's a good crowd tonight. I like the vibe, even when including all the firepower we travel with these days."

"Yeah. It's still the best place in town for people like us, or those who just feel different." Looking around, the manufactured fog on the floor and the multicolored laser lights were the same, but Chalky had added more security, and a few other patrons had private bodyguards as well. "And being different is becoming more dangerous every day."

She nodded, then turned to face him head on with a smile that slowly grew. "On a more personal note, since the news about you and Ens broke, I've been wondering..." Her tone softened as she continued. "Was it just me, or did I also detect a spark between *us*?"

He cleared his throat, feeling put on the spot and not liking it. "You're a lot like your mother, you know. You say what's on your mind.

Her grin grew. "So? Am I right?"

Adam felt his ears warming as his fingers tapped the table, knowing it was time to quit stalling. "Yes, and I'm glad to hear that you felt it, too. Sometimes I'm not sure if I can trust my instincts with women. I'm still new at this relationship stuff."

"Was it stronger with Ens?"

Opening his hands, he pleaded. "Come on, Maddy, there is no one else in my life like you two, and there never will be. Something spontaneous happened, and Ens and I aren't sure what comes next. This is going to be weird for all of us, but can we make it a little weird instead of a lot weird?"

Patting the table as if asking the dealer for another card, she laughed. "No worries, amigo. I just wanted to check to see if my gut was reading the chi between us correctly."

Over her shoulder he saw Ensley enter with the third set of armed guards. When she got to the table, she wasted no time, greeting him with a long, slow kiss. She grabbed his hand and then reached for Maddy's. "Who's ready for some fun tonight?"

With that they set out for the dance floor, sometimes dancing all together, but more often Maddy dancing with groups of fans while Adam and Ens paired. Around two in the morning, Maddy called it a night. "I promised mom we would write together to-morrow. I don't know how many more songs she has left in her, if you know what I mean."

After being offered encouragement that a cure would be found in time, Maddy headed out, leaving Adam and Ens alone in the crowded club. He wrapped her in his arms and swayed, eyes tenderly locked. "We can stay here in the city tonight, if you would like?"

Leaning closer, she kissed him. "I've been meaning to do some shopping, so staying here would save me some commuting time."

"How about we get out of here and see what comes next."

CHAPTER FORTY-FIVE

Callan drove toward a meeting in a shed beside an abandoned factory near Newark. He rarely smoked anymore, but today made an exception. *I've known Eddie and Al a long time. I'm not looking forward to this.* Arriving at his destination, he grabbed a Sig Sauer pistol from the center console. Exiting the SUV, he shoved it in his waistband, then took a final drag before flicking the cigarette butt on the ground, grinding it out in the loose gravel. *But in our business mistakes get you killed.*

He pulled the half-hinged metal door open, making a racket as he entered, spotting both men relaxing in cheap outdoor folding chairs. "Good to see you. Where's the punk?"

Eddie pointed to the door Callan had just walked through. "He's nervous as a cat. Said he needed some fresh air."

"Just as well, we need to talk without him around anyway."

Al finished his burger, then waded up the wrapper and tossed it into the debris pile in the corner. "Your message said you had a job for us." He laughed. "Been waiting to try out this Beretta nine mil."

"Nice." Callan moved closer, seeing an opportunity to make this unpleasant task easier. "Mind if I take a look?"

"Sure, boss. A new gun for a new job, just like you said."

Callan handled the weapon. "Glad you remembered that this time." He released the magazine, verifying the clip was full but the gun was unloaded, then slapped it back in. "I gave you guys the pistol I used on that African woman and told you to destroy it. You didn't, and it nearly caught up with us."

"It was a shortcut I'll never take again. I promise."

Still appearing to admire the gun, Callan turned toward Eddie. "And what were you two knuckleheads fighting about the other night, anyway?"

Eddie stared at his feet. "A stupid woman. Dipshit over there thought she should go home with him, but I'm the one who paid for all the drinks. If she was going home with anybody, it was going to be me."

"That was dumb." Chuckling, Callan asked. "Did you learn your lesson?"

"Yeah, boss. Never again."

His laughing stopped and his voice lowered. "You know what else was stupid?" It wasn't a question he expected them to answer. "Me bailing you out."

Eddie's eyebrows squished together. "Um, boss. I'm not following."

Callan sighed. "See, Eddie. When I bailed you out, someone identified me from the jail surveillance camera, and that's bad."

Al chimed in. "I get it, so you want us to go tie up that loose end."

Still holding the pistol, Callan discretely flicked the safety to the 'off' position. "Something like that." He paused and his eyes shot between the two of them, confirming their positions. "It's just that you two are the loose ends."

Recognition of what was about to happen seemed to dawn on them as they both tried to get out of the chairs. It was over quickly. Callan pulled the slide back, chambering the first round, then immediately fired a single bullet through Eddie's forehead, the chamber automatically reloading as the first casing ejected.

Trying to get away, Al had fallen getting out of his chair and began crawling away as fast as he could. It only delayed the inevitable by a couple of seconds as Callan sighted and fired a second shot through the back of Al's head.

The tight space had gone from pandemonium to calm in under five seconds, the only witness, it seemed, was the acrid smoke that filled the shed. Reaching down, he grabbed Al's chair and sat it upright. "Now I wait for the boy."

He took a seat in the man's chair and waited, finally deciding to light another cigarette. Blowing smoke, a thought occurred. *This has to be my last one for a while, or I'll be hooked again. These things will kill you.*

Phillip found his way back to the shed, saw another vehicle, and heard voices inside. He decided to peek through a hole in the corrugated metal of the flimsy building. *These guys scare me.*

He listened intently to their conversation, then watched in disbelief and horror as Callan gunned down two of his own men. Containing a scream, he turned and ran in a straight line as fast as he could toward a distant tree line, only pausing when he was deep inside dense woods. "What the fuck have I gotten myself into? They're stone-cold killers."

After catching his breath, he kept moving, not knowing where he was and not caring. All that mattered was putting space between himself and that man. Darkness began to fall, so he stopped beside a huge boulder. Mumbling, he made a decision. "It's too dark to keep going tonight. I'll hide here until morning."

In a black forest, he pulled his knees up close, wrapping them in his arms, trying to stay warm. The hoots of owls and snapping of twigs kept his nerves on edge, knowing this city boy wasn't alone in this wild place. His mind spun through what had happened. *I was relieved when Becky hooked me up with these guys, but now they want to kill me. Are her and Kelley down with that?*

Tears began. *I'm a murderer and I got my best friend killed. I'm so sorry, Anfernee.* He tried to stop the crying, but couldn't. *If that man finds me, I don't care. I deserve it.* Sobs convulsed his body through the dark night as the truth dawned. *There's no way this ends well for me.*

CHAPTER FORTY-SIX

Once again, Ansen awaited Dr. Chavez in his office, and once again he knew he would probably be more nervous than her. He heard the doorbell in the distance and checked his phone. "Ten o'clock. Right on time."

She had been shown to his office, but entered unannounced in trademark black slacks and blouse. "This is twice I've been summoned in a week. I have important work, so I hope this doesn't become a habit."

This is exactly why I want you on the council. I need someone clear-eyed who speaks the unvarnished truth. He did his best to relax, presenting what he hoped was an inviting smile. "Thank you for making time to see me, it means a lot." He motioned toward a pair of fronting sofas. "Please, join me."

Facing him, she wasted no time. "What's on your mind that we couldn't discuss on the phone? Seriously, I have a very important meeting in the city this afternoon."

Interlacing his fingers in his lap, he continued to smile, as much to calm himself in her presence as to project positivity. "I certainly respect your time, so I'll get down to business." His shoulders rose as he took in a quick breath. "As you know, a full council consists of a patriarch and twelve members."

"I know that, Ansen. What does that have to do with me?"

With her sharp reply, his smile felt fake, so he let it fade, matching her directness. "Imka is dead, and with Kristoff's passing, two seats are vacant. I need people I can trust."

Her laugh was the last thing he expected. "I appreciate your boldness, but do you know how many times I turned down Kristoff? I've always been a solo operator, and that's served me and the society well."

Ansen leaned forward, hand on his right knee, as he spoke in a low steady voice. "New threats are emerging with ties to the old reformers, and hard decisions need to be made. I respect the arrangement you had with Kristoff, but he's dead and times have changed. The society needs you on the council."

Leaning back, she smiled that crooked smile. "Looks like someone is growing into the job. I knew you were the right choice."

"So, you'll accept the offer?"

She crossed her arms. "You said something about the old reformers. What's that about?"

Sighing, he pushed back off his knee. "I thought I had heard the last of people named McDougal, Brown, and Slaughter. Yet those names popped up around the recent attacks in the city, including the assassination of Imka. We haven't put all the pieces together yet, but we're working on it."

Uncrossing her arms, Dr. Chavez's attitude seemed to change. "Oh? Do tell."

"We have evidence that connects Imka's assassination to the attempted murder of Madeline Blaze. And just a couple days ago, Callan McDougal was spotted bailing out two men from a New Jersey jail. That can't be a coincidence."

With a head tilt, she continued her inquiry. "And the other two names, Brown and Slaughter? How do they connect?"

Now it was Ansen who crossed his arms. "Seems the next generation is carrying similar grudges against us. Becky Brown and her wife, Kelley Slaughter are leaders of the WAGE movement, and now we know they were also involved in the attack on Adam. You remember the beating he received at the dance club, right?"

"Interesting."

"A good word choice." Ansen lowered his head. "And it gets more interesting because our three special children took matters into their own hands. They were the ones that identified Becky and Kelley, then roughed them up. Turns out, that's when our three got the first hints about the society, leading to their recent initiation."

Dr. Chavez's index finger now tapped her chin. "Very interesting."

Ansen again leaned toward her. "That's why I want you on the board. You know the threats and players on both sides better than anyone. Becky and Kelley may very well be connected to Callan, and that makes the situation even more dangerous. I'll give you just as much leeway to operate as you've had in the past, but the world and our society are in a delicate spot. No one else can add as much to our council as you. Will you answer the call this time?"

Her finger continued tapping as she appeared deep in thought until finally speaking. "I may be of assistance in this matter, whether I accept your offer or not."

"What do you mean?"

Curling on the right side, her crooked smile reemerged. "As you've acknowledged, I have been given wide latitude in society matters for a long time."

Ansen's memory snapped back to the moment he learned that he was Adam's father and her manipulation of the whole process. He didn't try to hide the sarcasm as he responded. "Yeah, I'm well aware."

She continued unfazed. "I've been working on another project which is about to come to fruition. I was planning to inform you when it was completed, but with what you've told me today, I realize the time is now...and you're really going to like what you're about to learn."

Once again, she had put him on edge. "Then by all means, tell me."

Eyes sparkling like a kid finally free to spill a great secret, her half-smile went full. "A young obstetrician was recently initiated into the society and contacted me with a request. She wanted to learn the techniques and skills of human genetic modification. As you might imagine, I get these requests all the time, so I ignored her until she dropped a couple of names. Care to guess who?"

It took a few seconds to process, then realization dawned. "Becky and Kelley? Are you serious?"

Like a proud lioness bringing home her prey, she confirmed his guess. "Exquisite, isn't it? Those two WAGE leaders are soon to be parents to a GM child."

Ansen was dumbfounded. "Why wasn't the council told?"

"The opportunity fell into my lap, and Kristoff agreed it was too good to pass up. We agreed that due to the sensitive nature of what we were doing, it would be our secret."

Like a bolt of lightning, Ansen recalled the virtual council meeting where they were put on hold as Kristoff took an urgent call. "So that's why he changed his plan."

"He was always imaginative in how we reach our goals."

"This gives us leverage." His thoughts leapt forward as if skipping the commercials of a TV recording. "Do they know?"

She scoffed. "Of course not. Where would the fun be in that?" Now she chuckled. "And you're correct. We do have leverage. They have an appointment with Dr. Simon next week. Would you like to join me to see their reaction when they find out?"

Sitting up straight, he gave a crisp nod. "I wouldn't miss it for the world." Hoping to capitalize on the triumphant mood, he pressed again. "This is exactly why you have to accept our offer."

Her eyes stared hard. "Do you swear I'll continue to have the same level of freedom?"

"You'll have the same level of autonomy as with Kristoff, while at the same time be privy to all inside information." He played to her ego. "Think of all you could accomplish."

He could almost see the gears turning as she considered the offer again. "Perhaps it is time to make my mark on the council."

"Yes...there's no one else who can do what you do."

Her nod was barely perceptible. "It is time to add to my legacy. Let the others know that I accept the invitation."

CHAPTER FORTY-SEVEN

Adam's second evening with Ensley surpassed their first, and cuddling in bed this morning stirred a depth of emotions he had never felt. *Is this what love feels like?*

True to her word, after a light breakfast Ensley headed out into one of the premier shopping capitols on the planet, with bodyguards in tow. He sat alone in his apartment and mused. *I'm the luckiest man in the world.* Before long, his thoughts drifted to the promise he made the evening before, to someone who clearly didn't feel the same. *I hope there's something I can do to help her.*

Pulling out his phone, he dictated a text. "How about Mario's, around the corner from Chalky's? One o'clock?"

In just a few seconds, a ping signaled her response. *Sounds good.*

After spending a few hours answering business emails, Adam made his way to the restaurant and as soon as he caught the distinctive smell of Mario's pizza crusts, his stomach growled. His protectors hung out by the door as he scanned the dining area. He spotted Kimee in a corner booth, almost not recognizing her with so little make-up. Making his way over, he weaved between crowded tables. "Hope you're as hungry as I am."

Her voice quivered. "Maybe not so much."

"What's wrong? It can't be that bad."

The waiter approached and Adam ordered a medium pepperoni pizza and a draft beer while Kimee selected an Italian vinaigrette salad with bread, and a water. As soon as he walked away, Adam continued. "Whatever it is, I bet we can figure something out."

The paper napkin she was holding looked as if had been through a shredder, and her face suddenly contorted as she put a hand to her mouth, then bolted toward the restroom. Adam sat alone until the food arrived, waiting for her return. *She's a wreck. Now I'm even more worried about her.*

A few minutes later, she sat back down at the table, face pale and blotchy. "Sorry about that. My emotions are all over the place lately."

He reached for her hand, which felt cold and clammy. "Eat some bread. It will settle your stomach."

Taking his advice, she pulled little pieces from the fresh loaf as he wolfed down his first bites. "Mmm. Mario's pizza tastes as good at one in the afternoon as it does at one in the morning." Finishing his first slice, he washed it down with half of his cold beer. "Want to try again? Is it school? Money problems?" He wiped his mouth with one of the thin paper napkins. "I'm sure there's something we can do."

The cheeks that had been so ashen, now blushed. "This isn't easy to tell you... I just hope you won't hate me."

"I could never hate you, we're friends. You can trust me."

Her chin trembled. "Okay, then I'm just going to say it." She pulled another napkin from the dispenser and dabbed under her glassy eyes, then spoke just above a whisper. "I'm pregnant."

Adam sat stunned, as if hit by a blast of Artic air in July. He leaned toward her. "Did you say you're pregnant?"

Kimee nodded twice. "I was on the pill, but when I looked it up, I found that in real life it's only ninety-one percent effective. Guess I'm one of the unlucky nine percenters."

Now he was the one whose stomach churned. "Are we here

today because it's... mine?"

Again, she nodded twice. "I'm sorry."

Finishing his beer, Adam signaled the waiter for another, then turned back to Kimee with a tremble now creeping into his voice. "What are you...we... going to do?" The second beer arrived, and the waiter left without saying a word, perhaps sensing the tension of the moment.

"That's all I've been thinking about since I missed my period. After a positive test, I went to a clinic to talk with a counselor, but that's not the way I was raised. At the same time, I'm a single woman barely making ends meet. I can't raise a kid on my own, so I've been looking into giving it up for adoption."

Struggling with the news, he questioned. "Are you sure, really sure it's mine?"

Her bloodshot eyes glared. "I may dress sexy, but I don't sleep around... usually. I've not been with anyone else in months. If I decide to go through with this, we'll have it tested when it's born, but trust me, it's yours."

Adam realized how hurtful his words were. "Hey, I'm sorry. This just came out of the blue and I'm trying to get my bearings, okay?"

Her shoulders slouched. "It's a lot, isn't it?"

A tear trickled down her cheek, so he handed her another napkin, as his world spun. "You would really give up your... *our* child?"

Her body shook as she talked. "Look, my father left us when I was three, and mom and I have lived paycheck to paycheck ever since. I don't have many options."

While he had just found out he would be a father, he knew that he had options. He gently put his hand atop hers resting on the table. "However you choose to proceed will be your decision, I get that. But if you choose to have this child, I'll be the father both genetically and financially, you and the baby will be taken care of. You have my word on that."

Seconds turned to minutes as she wept with her head bowed. When she looked up, her splotchy face glistened from the flood of salty tears. "I hope you know I never wanted to have this conversation with you, or anyone else for that matter. Ever." She leaned back, pulling her hand from his. "I hate being in this jam."

Her minutes of silence had given Adam time to gather his thoughts. "I'm still processing this, but I do know a thing or two about pregnancies from all the conversations I've had about designer babies. I don't know how this is going to work, but *we* will figure it out. You're not alone in the world."

Kimee rubbed her eyes. "God, my life is so jacked up." More thin napkins were sacrificed in the effort to dry her face. "I still don't know exactly what I'm going to do, but I'll let you know soon, okay?"

"Sure, when you're ready." He touched her hand again. "Can I ask a favor?"

She deposited the damp napkin on the growing pile. "I guess."

He felt awkward asking, but did it anyway. "Until you decide, can we keep this on the DL. If you decide to keep it, I've got some people to prepare."

Her words sounded cold and flat. "You mean like your girlfriend?"

A head tilt signaled his shame. "That won't be an easy conversation, but it won't even register on the Richter scale compared to the one I'll have with my parents. Unplanned pregnancies seem to rattle them."

CHAPTER FORTY-EIGHT

Ansen paced while he and Dr. Chavez waited alone in Dr. Simon's office. She was down the hall in one of the clinic's exam rooms with Becky and Kelley, following their unexpected call requesting to be seen before their next scheduled appointment only a few days away. He stopped in front of her. "Any idea what's got them so scared they came out of hiding?"

Her laugh signaled she knew. "No matter how many times Dr. Simon told them their baby's growth was just the result of being a big fetus, they're not stupid. They *want* to believe it, badly, but in their gut, they know something's off."

A flashback of the look on Bree's face upon finding out about her nine-week pregnancy timeline five years ago, chilled him. "Is it the same schedule you used with us?"

She waved him off. "Not exactly. They would have found out before totally bonding with the child and would have considered an abortion. I couldn't allow that, so they're on a more moderate six-month schedule, meaning the baby should arrive in the next seven-to-ten days."

While he was glad to be gaining leverage with these two women, he was simultaneously impressed and repulsed at the ease with which Chavez manipulated people. *Glad she's on my side.* That thought triggered another. "While we have a moment, what's the update on helping Gwen and Ray?"

Shaking her head, she frowned. "We've made progress, but I'm afraid it may be too little too late. Just between us, Ray has told me he's experiencing some symptoms as well."

"Damn. That's not what I wanted to hear. After all we've been through, they're more like family than friends."

Before Dr. Chavez could reply, Dr. Simon entered the room. "We're ready for you two."

Chavez stood. "What have you told them?"

"We've completed the ultrasound and I reassured them their baby is healthy."

Ansen nodded. "That's good. How are we to be introduced?"

Dr. Simon rubbed her hands together, clearly not as comfortable deceiving patients as the other doctor in the room. "I told them there happens to be a couple of experts visiting the clinic today who could answer their questions better than me. They are waiting anxiously."

"I love this part." Smiling, Dr. Chavez continued. "It never gets old. Let's go rock their world."

Following Dr. Simon, they made their way to the third exam room on the left. Upon entering, Dr. Simon started to introduce the two 'experts.' "I would like you both to meet…"

Becky jumped to her feet shouting. "I know who you are, both of you! What the hell's going on here?"

Chavez took charge, stepping in front of the visibly shaken, Dr. Simon. "Open your eyes. You're two smart women, what do you think's going on?"

A swarm of emotions seemed to run across both Becky and Kelley's faces as they processed the situation, then Kelley began crying. Becky's fist clenched and she took a step toward Dr. Simon.

Ansen saw the aggressive move and cut her off. "Step back, or you'll have me to deal with."

Looking up at the much larger man, her face burned fire engine red. "Somebody better start talking or I swear I'll destroy this place!"

"Sit down and shut up." Dr. Chavez was now in control as she put her arm around Dr. Simon's shoulder. "It's simple. You wanted a perfect baby and my new friend wanted to learn the most advanced techniques in the field."

Becky kept an arm around the now bawling Kelley as she shouted even louder. "You traitor! We trusted you and you betrayed us! We'll have your license!"

Dr. Chavez laughed almost as loud as Becky had screamed. "Really? And what will you do when your relationship with that wanted killer, Phillip Poppins, is revealed?"

Bulging eyes glared back. "You wouldn't dare."

"Or maybe when you have this special child in a week or so, we'll leak a story to the *Times* that two of leaders of WAGE decided to have a designer baby of their own. We'll tell them you tried to keep it hidden." Dr. Chavez scoffed. "How do you think that will play with your supporters?"

Becky's bottom lip trembled and her voice shook. "A week? We should have three more months. You bastards!"

With a regal gaze, Dr. Chavez sneered. "I've been called far worse. You'll have to do better than that to impress me."

The woman who moments ago was raging, now cowered with her wife. "You're a monster." She then shot a defeated stare at Ansen. "Both of you."

Returning the glare and adding a pointed finger, Ansen replied. "And what kind of person are you to hit my son in the head with a crowbar?"

Tears now flowed from both women as Kelley whimpered. "What are you going to do to us, to this baby? Are you going to kill us?"

Ansen stepped closer. "As you're about to find out, we're not the brutes you think we are. We're not going to do anything to you or your child."

"What's the catch?" Sounding weak and overwhelmed Becky continued. "When a deal is too good to be true, there are always strings attached."

"You're a smart woman, Becky Brown." Ansen knelt down to eye level. "Because there *are* stipulations, starting with telling us where we can find Phillip Poppins."

Becky had stopped crying and sniffed as she rubbed her right eye with the back of her hand. "Honestly, we don't know. We got him hooked up with someone who can keep him hidden and out of jail. I wouldn't be surprised if he were out of the country by now."

Ansen smiled confidently. "Would that someone be Callan McDougal?"

Her eyes widened. "How do you know him?"

"The question is, how do *you* know him?"

The pair sat silently huddled, then Becky straightened and looked Ansen in the eye. "That's an interesting story, one that will cost you something in return, if you want to hear it."

Standing back up, Ansen shook his head. "I've heard stories of the legendary Ben Brown. Stories of his dogged determination and fearlessness. The acorn seems not to have fallen far from the tree. If the tale is good enough, we can make a deal. What do you want?"

Becky stood, facing Ansen with a spark in her delivery. "First of all, we want to protect the privacy of our baby. No one can know his genome has been modified."

"We're listening. What else."

Taking a quick glance at Kelley, she continued. "And we need to remain employed at WAGE, at least for a little while. It's our only source of income and we'll need some time to transition out."

Ansen couldn't believe what he was hearing. "You do know that every success you have there will harm your child, and mine."

"Let us figure that out. We just need some time."

"What else is on your growing list?"

Becky took in a sharp breath. "We're going to have some serious security concerns in the very near term. We'll need society level protection, or there's no deal."

A single laugh escaped Ansen's lips. "You have some big asks on your list. What makes you so sure your information is worth it?"

She looked him up and down. "I'm surprised. You seem like an honest man, and I didn't expect that. So, here's the offer. I'll tell you what I know and after hearing me out, if you can look me in the eye and tell me it wasn't worth it, then we'll live with the consequences. Deal?"

"You seem pretty confident."

"I am."

Ansen glanced at Dr. Chavez, who shrugged her shoulders, then added her analysis. "Either way, we get the information."

He turned to the pair. "Alright, we have a deal. This better be good."

Kelley reached for Becky's hand. "Are you sure you know what you're doing? This could get us killed."

Becky held her wife tight. "As I see it, our back's already against the wall. This might be our only way out. Besides, deep down I've wanted revenge on her since my father's death." She faced Ansen. "You have a snake in your midst. Liza Howard is my connection with Callan McDougal."

Ansen's jaw dropped. "That traitor!"

Grinning, Becky stuck her hand out. "I see we have a deal."

CHAPTER FORTY-NINE

It had taken Phillip three days to walk the eighteen miles from Newark to Ft. Lee New Jersey, and it hadn't been an easy trip. He didn't have any cash on him when he went underground, and he knew better than to use a credit card. To avoid being tracked, Callan had destroyed his phone the moment they met, so he couldn't call anyone to come get him. Besides, he was having a tough time deciding who he could trust. His mind had played out multiple scenarios and always arrived at the same conclusion. *Becky and Kelley set me up. They had to know of Callan's plan to kill me. There's no other way.*

He stayed hidden most of each day, coming out only as darkness fell on the Garden State. Once on the move, dumpster diving for food and avoiding the police were his priorities. His mood went from bleak to black as he traveled. *I feel like a filthy rat, hiding from killer cats.*

On the second day of the journey, he dreamed of Anfernee as he slept in the small space between a roadway overpass and its concrete supports. Exhaustion, hunger and being off his meds fed visions as he and his dead friend discussed how Phillip should end his suffering. From beyond the grave Anfernee summed up the options. "No way you survive prison, they would pass you around like a two-bit whore, so that leaves you two choices. Run like a coward until that Callan dude catches up with you, or take matters into your own hands and go out in a blaze of glory."

When he woke he mumbled to himself. "Blaze of glory it is."

Now with a purpose, he spent the remainder of the walk back

to the city developing the plan, and by the time he stood at the foot of the George Washington bridge it was fully formed. His energy level rose with each step over the Hudson, and when he set foot back in the city, he was ready. *The world will know Phillip Poppins!*

While getting back to New York was an accomplishment, there was still much to do, and he talked to himself as he walked from Washington Heights into Manhattan. "First, surveil the warehouse. The police or that Callan guy might be waiting for me." One step at a time, he made his way, mumbling like a homeless man. "If the coast is clear, a shower. God, it will feel good to be clean again."

Turning from W. 179th street onto Broadway he continued his muttering monologue. "A change of clothes, then money from the safe and I'm out of there. It's risky to stay in one place for too long." He stopped and waited until the traffic light changed. Walking again, his plan continued to roll out. "Got to get a couple of slices from Geno's... hell, I'm buying a whole pie, then I'll find a nice spot in Central Park to enjoy it."

From Broadway he turned at St. Nicholas Avenue. "When I'm good and full I'll head down to Johnny Smooth's gun shop. Like last time, I'll flash some bills and get invited to the special back room. Cash is king down there." He laughed lightly. "For a couple of days, I'll party like there's no tomorrow, then I'll do the deed and be hailed as a king... unless you're a freak, of course."

Taking side streets, he did a covert scan around all sides of his building, and deciding it was safe, he entered through the back door. Feeling good about himself for the first time in days he spoke aloud in the large open space. "The world will know Phillip Poppins!" His words echoed off the concrete block walls, then he continued. "Anfernee, it won't be long!"

He heard his dead friend's reply as clearly as he had heard his own words. "I'm waiting on the other side!"

CHAPTER FIFTY

Now back in their Malibu home, Gwen woke in a foul mood. Walking out of the house wearing only a skimpy, nearly see-through pink pajama set, she headed along the curved pathway to Ray's onsite lab. Her eyes were wide, scanning for assassins she thought were closing in, screaming the whole way. "Where's that god-damned cure you keep promising?"

Ray seemed ready for her rants as his researchers looked on. "We're making so much progress, especially with insights from Dr. Chavez's team. Gwen, I promise you'll be the first to know when it's ready. Trust me, we're working as hard as we can."

"Shit, Ray. If you don't hurry up, I'm going to have to come down here and whip some of these egghead's asses. I mean it! You know I will!"

He moved closer, wrapping her small frame completely in his embrace, his voice breaking. "You're as tough as they come. I'll crack the whip and make sure everybody's working even faster, so you don't have to come in here again. We're going to get this done."

The words comforted her but her mood swung from anger to despair as suddenly as a car speeding around a hairpin curve on the canyon road. Through sobs she confessed. "I don't know how long I can hold on. What I do know is I can't go on like this much longer."

Smoothing her hair, he made a suggestion. "How about we go back to the house, get you dressed and make you some break-fast? Maybe an egg white omelet?"

With her head buried in his chest she nodded. "Yeah, that sounds nice." Her voice cracked with emotion.

∞

When Ray returned an hour later, he made an announcement to his team. "Sorry you had to see that again. It's been a rough few days."

Martin, his senior researcher, approached. "Must be tough on you when she doesn't even remember she did the same thing yesterday, and the day before."

A weariness seemed to inhabit every cell of his body. "I'm worried about her. She's mentioning suicide more often."

"This disease sucks so bad a quarter of sufferers consider it."

Ray patted his shoulder. "That's why we really do have to go faster. Her case is accelerating quicker than almost any I've ever seen, and she's always been a very determined woman."

CHAPTER FIFTY-ONE

Adam read the text from Kimee that he had been expecting. *I'm keeping the baby.*

He quickly tapped his reply. *We'll do this together, and figure it out as we go.* He was smart enough to build a business plan for a bank that had gone global, but lacked the experience or maturity to know what the arrival of this baby would actually mean to either of their lives. But of one thing he was sure, he would do his best for this coming child.

She replied in a one letter answer. *K*

He slid his phone back in his pocket when he heard Ensley call from the kitchen. "What's up?"

Closing his eyes and taking in a deep breath, he prepared himself for a conversation he never expected. Joining her, he headed for the fridge. "Glass of wine?"

"A little early, isn't it?"

Glancing at the microwave clock and seeing it was not yet ten in the morning, he shrugged. "Not today." He looked up at the ceiling for a moment, then slowly lowered his gaze until meeting her eyes. "There's something I need to tell you."

"I don't like the sound of that." She crossed her arms. "Am I going to need a drink too?"

"Definitely." He filled two stemmed glasses nearly to the brim with chilled chardonnay, then carefully carried them to the table. "And you're going to want to sit down."

Taking a seat, she pushed a stray strand of coal black hair behind her ear. "I'm not going to like this, am I?"

Adam stared at the table. "I'm not going to like saying it, and you're not going to like hearing it." He took a long sip, then continued as she seemed to study his face. "I messed up, and I need to be the one who tells you before you find out some other way."

"It can't be that bad…can it?" Her words sounding equal parts curious and cautious.

Tilting his head, he blew out a loud sigh. "I'll let you answer that after I tell you." He took another sip. "Do you remember that time Kiss Me Kimee kissed Maddy?"

"Yeah. What about it? She kissed me once, too."

He drummed his fingers a couple of time. "Well, one night she kissed me as well." His statement was met by silence and narrowing eyes. "First, you need to know this happened before you and I were…" He paused because they still hadn't labeled their new relationship. "Before you and I were you and I."

"Is it still going on?" Her question was spoken cold, without emotion.

"No." Now it was her turn to drink while he fidgeted, finally getting the words out. "It was a one-night thing." His gaze broke away as he looked out the window in a blinkless stare. "At least we both thought it was."

"What's changed?" A quiver shaped her response.

A question answered a question. "Did you know that the pill isn't one-hundred percent effective?"

"She's not…"

"Yes…she is."

"Damn it, Adam!"

He hung his head in shame. "I know. Like I said, I messed up."

Rapid fire questions bombarded him. "Are you sure it's yours?

What's she going to do? What are you going to do?" He thought she was done, then one more bombshell landed. "And what about us?"

His head jerked up. "Please Ens. Like I said this happened before you and I got together. You can ask her yourself, it was a one-night thing, and we both knew it."

"Leave me out of this! I'm not asking her anything. It's going to be weird enough just seeing her at Chalky's." They both took a long drink as an unsettled silence filled the room. When she spoke again the coldness returned. "So, what's next?"

With eyes closed, he rubbed his forehead. "I found out today she's going to keep it... swears it's mine. We'll have it tested when it's born, of course, but she says there was no one else, sooo..."

"What does she want?"

"Nothing." Adam sighed heavily. "I'm going to do the right thing financially, but that's about as far as I've figured out." He shook his head. "What a mess."

"Who else knows?"

"I think it's just her mom and us, but soon enough mother nature will out us."

"Speaking of mothers," Ensley laughed derisively. "When are you going to tell yours? She'll blow a fuse."

He rubbed his head again. "I'm heading there next. Want to come for moral support, or just to watch the fireworks?"

Her jaw went slack and she sounded incredulous. "Are you serious? I don't want to be anywhere near this train wreck. You're on your own, lover boy."

He felt sick. "Ens, please know this was an accident, and I'm sorry. The timing sucks, but I can't change what's happened. I can only move forward, and I would like to continue doing that with you."

She drained her glass, then stood. "Right now, I need some time to think. It's going to take a while for me to sort out how I feel about this whole affair."

Joining her in standing, Adam reached for her hand, which she jerked away. "Ens, please!"

"Give me some space...I think we need to take a break from each other for a while."

"Wait!"

Putting her hand up, she snapped. "Just stop!" Her voice lowered. "I'll touch base in a few days."

With that she turned and walked out the door. Adam went to the balcony and watched from above as she exited the building with her two body guards. He ran a hand through his hair. *Well, that could have gone better.* He watched as her black SUV pulled away. *And I know it will only be worse when I tell mom and dad.*

CHAPTER FIFTY-TWO

Maddy had returned from her trip to write with her mother. Because of the increased security, she had taken up the offer from Adam's parents to stay on their estate. She was surprised when Adam asked her to sit in on a family meeting. "Why do you want me there?"

Looking like a teen who had wrecked the family car, he answered mysteriously. "I want a witness in case they decide to kill me."

"What?"

He seemed on edge. "Look, this is something you need to know too, and there's no reason to tell the sad tale twice."

When Adam said the word 'pregnant' she realized why he wanted her there. *Adam. What the hell?* She sat back, trying to become invisible as his mother flipped out.

"You know the world is watching you almost every minute of the day." She had never heard Mrs. Battle yell so loud. "What the hell were you thinking?"

Adam's father took over the interrogation with just as much vigor and volume, the only difference being his voice was a lower pitch. "Who is this girl? Are you sure it's yours? What does she want? What are you going to do?"

Like a boxer being pummeled, Adam did his best to fend off the blows. "Her name is Kimee. We'll do a DNA test to confirm. I'm still figuring that out."

Maddy leaned forward as his mother tagged back in, bringing up a subject she had not yet considered, but really wanted to hear his answer to. "And what about you and Ensley? What does she have to say about all this?"

Watching Adam fall back in his chair, she knew that punch landed the hardest. "I told her a couple of hours ago and it went a whole lot like this." He crossed his arms and finished his answer just above a whisper. "She says we're taking a break until she figures some things out."

"Damn it, Adam." Ms. Battle sounded less angry now, but just as frustrated. "This is a debacle of your own making...but we'll figure it out." Her frustration now morphed into motherly support. "I'm disappointed in your judgment, but you know we love you. We'll get through this together."

His father traced a similar path. "Your actions are bringing an unplanned new life into this world. Promise us you won't do something else stupid to fuck it up worse." Walking over to his son, he put a hand on his shoulder, seeming to try and bring some perspective to the situation. "Your mother's pregnancy with you wasn't easy and we made it through everything. We'll have your back and do what's right for this baby."

After the family meeting finished, Maddy followed Adam outside as his head hung low. When they were out of earshot of his parents, she patted his back. "Whoa. My mom curses all the time, especially now, but your folks know how to use all those words, too. They tore you a new one."

Her words had the intended effect as he laughed a little. "Yeah, but I deserved it. This is going to be a royal mess."

They walked aimlessly until she pulled a joint out her pocket. She smiled like the little devil in cartoons that sits on people's shoulders and tempts them. "Want to feel a little better about life?"

His eyes widened. "There's a big rock beside a stream just over this knoll." He smiled for the first time since his arrival. "You're a lifesaver."

They each took a couple of hits, then she brushed the fire off the end. "That should take the edge off for a while."

He lay back on the huge sun-warmed stone as the buzz kicked in for them both and the sun began slipping below the skyline. "My life's never going to be the same, is it?"

"Lighten up, Adam. It's not like you're the first person to have this kind of thing happen." She now reclined beside him and stared at the gradually darkening sky, spying the first twinkle of a star. "We're young, wealthy and famous, and what Shakespeare once said applies to us. 'The world is your oyster."

"I know you're right, but I made a mess of my life as well as Kimee's, and things are jacked up between Ens and me right now. It's all my fault. Just because we have terrific lives, doesn't mean things are always perfect."

She felt philosophical as the buzz leveled. "Let's take that all apart, amigo. The way I heard the story, Kimee owned that night just as much as you, right?"

He seemed to ponder her point of view. "Well...I guess you're right. We both made choices that we'll live with."

Now up on an elbow, she spoke sincerely. "I'm sure Ens will get over it, too. You two seem to have a good thing going."

He shook his head. "You didn't see how she left it. I'm not sure we'll ever be the same."

She first reassured. "I bet she'll be back in no time and you two will work things out." Her buzz gave her the courage to say something she had felt for a while, but never acted on. "But if she doesn't, maybe we'll find out how *our* chi meshes." Seeing surprise in his eyes, she acted before losing her nerve, kissing him gently.

She could see his blush, even in the fading light as he lay silent with a curious smile. "That was unexpected...and very nice, but-"

The ringing of her phone with her father's ringtone interrupted the moment, and she bolted upright. "I have to take this. Dad almost never calls." Feeling suddenly sober, she answered anxiously. "Dad? What's up."

His voice was shaky. "Are you somewhere safe?"

The odd question caused her spine to stiffen. "Yes. I'm hanging out with Adam at his folk's place. What's wrong?"

"Good." Now he sounded as if he could barely get the words from his mouth. "It's your mother..."

"What's wrong with mom! Talk to me dad! What's happening!" She imagined a fall down the marble stairs. "Tell me she's alright!"

"She took some pills..."

Panic grew exponentially, setting her brain on fire. "Tell me! Tell me she's going to be okay!!"

Hearing him weeping from their California home, she knew the truth before he spoke the words. "The paramedics did all they could... but she's gone."

Maddy screamed into the enveloping darkness. "Nooooo!!!"

Adam could hear only one side of the conversation, but seemed to pick up on what was happening as he put an arm around her. "I'm here for you."

She heard her father's voice attempting to comfort her from afar but couldn't process what he was saying, her mind in overdrive but simultaneously paralyzed. Her body felt numb as she finally processed a fragment. "... we'll get through this..." A surging emotional tidal wave broke through as violent sobs shook her and the phone slipped from her hand.

Steadying Maddy while retrieving the phone, Adam put the call on speaker. "This is Adam. Are you alright, Mr. Manza?"

"I'm so glad Maddy is with her friends. We're dealing with a tragedy, and if I can't be there for her, I'm glad you are."

Sobbing morphed into wails of despair and Adam pulled her closer. "I'm so sorry, sir. We'll take care of Maddy here, and get her to you as soon as we can." With final goodbyes said, the call ended.

Maddy's body shook uncontrollably, and she didn't care. "I knew things were tough for her lately, but I thought we had more time."

He held her. "She knew how much you loved her."

The tears seemed to flow from a bottomless well. "I should have been there with her. Maybe I could have done something, said something."

"Don't go there, Maddy. Something bad happened, but this isn't your fault."

She leaned into his embrace, glad to have a friend with her she knew she could count on. "Why, Adam. Why!!!" It was now almost completely dark, and it felt like sorrow was squeezing her insides. Her lungs burned and her stomach churned. He held her as she screamed one last denial against the gathering gloom. "NOOO!!!"

CHAPTER FIFTY-THREE

Blaming Becky and Kelley for at least part of his circumstances, Phillip turned to the solace of the drugs that once had nearly killed him. The events of the past three days had been powered by heroin and cocaine, as he struggled to dull the pain of Becky and Kelley's betrayal. *How could my friends treat me like this?* The initial euphoria of the heroin rush was followed by warm sensations of safety, which was the exact opposite of what he felt when his mind replayed Callan killing those two men. *I'm a walking dead man.*

But the heroin slowed him down and he needed to have energy for this task, so he snorted another line of coke. The rush was intense and his heartrate increased, causing him to announce his feeling of power inside the car. "No one can stop me!"

Parking the barely drivable junker half-a-block away from Chalky's, a thought popped into his mind. *My face is surely on a wanted poster somewhere.* A crazed wobbly smile formed. *I wish I could have seen it.* He reassured himself aloud. "Maybe in the next life."

Reaching into the back seat, Phillip pulled the AK up front, double checking the clip. Satisfied his weapon was ready, he reviewed the plan. *Too bad those three are in California for that sleazy singer's mother's funeral. I would wait for their return, but I swear I can feel that Callan guy's aura getting closer. On the plus side that means a little less security in the place.*

Cutting another line on the small cracked windowpane he

found on the floor of the abandoned building in which he had slept last night, he wasted no time snorting the white powder through the last twenty-dollar bill to his name. "The only good Freaker is a dead Freaker!"

His mind now raced faster, in sync with his accelerated pulse. *Two guards outside means I'll be shooting my way in. Once inside, just do as much damage as I can, hoping I have time to use both clips before the bullet with my name finds me. If I can take out that Chalky guy and at least twenty others, then I'll become a legend.*

There was enough drug left on the square for one more line. As he moved the powder on the glass, another thought occurred. *If I used this credit card in a store, it would be flagged before I could get around the corner. Cutting cocaine is all it's good for.* Taking the rolled up twenty between his fingers he snorted one last time.

Finishing, he slung the cracked glass square toward the passenger side floor where it shattered on impact. "Fucking yeah! Time to make history!"

He slammed his palms on the steering wheel five times in rapid succession, pumping himself up even farther. Flinging the door open, he stepped out, his canvas black duster giving him a Wild West appearance. "Here I come!"

Now out in the open he began to trot, speeding up as he got closer until breaking into a full run with the rifle up to his shoulder. Seeing one of the guards at the door reach for a gun, Phillip fired first, taking out both sentinels as bystanders scattered. "Run, you little Freaker shits!" He shot again, taking two of them down.

Wasting no time, he burst through the door and saw the mass of people running for the back exits. He unloaded into their backs taking down as many as he could before the first clip emptied. Switching to the second one took less than five seconds and he began firing again, but now looking for a specific target.

Spying Chalky, his finger squeezed until the owner of the club lay bleeding on the dance floor. Sensing there might be a chance for him to survive after all, he turned toward the entrance, running, until he saw a cute girl frozen in place near the hostess stand. He fired at her, laughing. "One more dead freak!"

A second later he heard the sound of another gun and felt a hard strike to the back of his head, and in that instant, as his life-force blinked out, he knew the name Phillip Poppins would live on in infamy.

CHAPTER FIFTY-FOUR

The day of Gwen Blaze's memorial service was the saddest day of Adam's life, and in talking with Maddy and Ensley he found it the same for them. Besides the obvious tragedy of Maddy's mother passing, they had learned of the massacre at Chalky's. They sat on folding chairs on the beach as some new age Guru named Baba Mashni blabbered on about karma and nirvana and reincarnation, trying to make the living feel better about the terrible events that had taken place.

It wasn't working for Adam. He had been casting about in an emotional sea, trying to process the destruction and deaths of those who meant so much to him. He recited their names in his mind like a non-stop chant as the Guru continued. *Yori, Chalky, Kimee... a child yet to be named. Yori, Chalky, Kimee... a child yet to be named. Yori, Chalky, Kimee... a child yet to be named.*

After some of Gwen Blaze's ashes had been scattered in the waves, family and friends made their way back up to the former singer's cliff-side home. Maddy stood by her father accepting mourner's condolences as Adam and Ens went out to the pool deck. A light breeze ruffled his hair. "How's Maddy doing?"

"She's beyond numb, but desperate to publicly hold it together for her father." Ens sighed. "I can't begin to imagine..."

Adam gave life to a vendetta. "Someone's going to pay for what happened at Chalky's."

She reached for his hand. "It was horrific, but you heard what our parents said. Let the society handle it."

Looking out over the waves below, he spoke in a low growl.

"They killed Yori, Chalky, Kimee… and my unborn child. Other than my family and you and Maddy, those are the people that meant the most to me, and now they're gone. Fuck what my folks say. This is personal."

Ensley moved to face him, taking both hands as she pleaded. "Give them a chance, please. The gunman is dead… and they say he was alone."

"He's one of the punks who ran with Becky Brown. You know as well as I do that she is involved. She's the brains of the bunch."

Tugging at his hands she seemed to switch tactics. "Right now, we're on the west coast, so there's nothing we can do about it. What we can do is go back inside and support Maddy. These past few days have been awful for her."

Thinking of their friend, he stood close beside Ensley, looking through the big windows framing Maddy and her father inside. "I heard they ruled it an accidental overdose…and while easier to understand than suicide, it doesn't change the hurt they must be feeling."

"She was so close to her mother… almost like sisters. They wrote together, recorded together, even toured together. Her parents were right to do the rapid maturation gene edits, otherwise Maddy would hardly have any memories of her mom."

Adam watched as yet another person shook Ray's hand. "Let's hope Dr. Chavez and Mr. Manza can find the cure soon, otherwise Maddy's going to be all alone in the world."

Ensley put an arm around Adam. "She'll never be alone, as long as we're alive."

He liked the sensation of having her close again and reciprocated, putting his arm around her. "I know this isn't good timing, but I'll ask anyway. Any chance we can ever be good again?"

She leaned, resting her head against his ribcage in the crook of his embrace. "Funerals have a way of making me take stock of my own life. You screwed up, and I judged you harshly. But with everything that's happened I realize that life's too short to let one mistake derail our happiness."

He smiled for the first time in days. "I'm glad to hear that. I'll try to stay out of trouble from now on."

Now she poked him in the side. "That better include letting the society deal with Becky Brown and her crew. Promise?"

Nodding, he shaded the truth, not telling her he had already contacted Silverstone Confidential asking them to locate and surveil them. "I'll stay out of it… for now."

"Good. Revenge has a way of scarring the giver as much as the receiver. Now, let's go in there and support our Maddy, like best friends should."

CHAPTER FIFTY-FIVE

Once back in New York, Ansen set about the task of dealing with the traitor in their midst. With the events of the past few days there was a new urgency to his darkened mood. *I can't believe she sat right next to me at the last video council meeting. Right here in my home.* Another video call was about to begin, and he knew this one would be tense. *No one wants to be used as bait...but somebody has to do it. And after what their friend did, they're in no position to object.*

The link connected, and Ansen saw two faces staring back from Becky's phone from their safehouse. "Becky, Kelley. Good morning."

Their joint reply sounded frosty. "Hello."

"So much for your friend, Phillip, being out of the country." Ansen leaned closer to the screen. "He really made a mess of things."

Becky replied forcefully, but without looking directly into the camera. "You can't pin that on us. He had issues and spun out of control." Her eyes drifted up toward the lens. "But yes. He sure fucked things up."

Ansen's voice lowered. "I'll take your word you didn't know, but there's something else that makes his actions even worse. One of the young women killed was carrying my grandchild. This tragedy is both public and personal."

Both women's eyes opened wide as Becky continued as spokesperson. "Like I said. We had nothing to do with that, nothing. In fact, it hurts us as well. Our faces have been all over the news as associates of his, and donations to WAGE have fallen by more than thirty percent in less than a week."

Crossing his arms, Ansen continued. "As bad as that situation is, you know it's not the reason for this call." He stared into the camera. "It's time to chop the head off the snake."

"Hey, wait a minute. We had a deal."

"And we've honored that deal. No one knows about your child's genome, and you're still at WAGE." He paused. "And today we talk about society protection for what comes next."

Kelley finally spoke. "I thought that was all society business. Why even involve us?"

Just the thought of Liza's betrayal made his jaw stiffen. "She's talked her way out of too many tight spots to count, so I need to catch her in an act of treachery. Something so audacious she seals her own fate."

Becky again spoke for the couple. "What are you purposing?"

"I'm going to set a trap, with you two as bait."

They looked at each other as Kelley shook her head. "I don't like the sound of that. She's a dangerous woman."

Ansen fired back. "That's precisely why we need to take her down, once and for all."

Becky's lips pursed. "That's not part of the deal. Count us out."

"You misunderstand." Ansen's eyes bore holes through the lens, transmitting his anger all the way to the hideout. "This is not a negotiation. I'm setting the trap using you as the bait whether you like it or not. Liza *is* going to come gunning for you today. Your choice is to play along while the society guarantees your safety, or face her on your own."

Becky glanced at Kelley and shrugged her shoulder, reaching the only decision he knew they could. "What do you need us to do?"

Ansen's anger retreated as he replied. "It's easy. Don't do anything except stay in that cabin until you get further instructions. The snake will slither to you."

CHAPTER FIFTY-SIX

Liza wasn't surprised by the invitation to join Ansen at his home for another virtual council meeting. *After what went down at that night club, I'm sure his feathers are ruffled.* Whatever the case, it was another opportunity to keep her finger on the pulse of things as she plotted her takeover. *He should just be thankful that awful singer died, so his genetically twisted son was out of town, and not among the dead.*

The car arrived, and she was shown to Ansen's office, and immediately oozed fake sympathy. "Ansen, I was so sorry to hear of Gwen's passing. Your families are so close. It's a real tragedy for the world."

"Thank you, Liza. It has been a tough stretch." He motioned to the chair beside his. "I've got a lot going on today, so let's bring up the rest of the members." With a few keystrokes, the faces broadcasting from around the globe were brought up on his screen. "It is with a heavy heart that I welcome everyone."

Charlotte spoke first from Sydney. "I think I can speak for all when I say how saddened we were, hearing of the passing of Gwen Blaze, especially as she was so recently initiated."

A chorus of agreement filtered in as Liza's serene visage never changed. *Speak for yourself.*

"It was indeed a sad day. She did so much good for all of our special children long before she even knew of our existence. Her influence will be missed." Ansen moved to change the subject. "But on more happy news, I'm pleased to welcome Dr. Cielo Chavez to our council. Everyone knows how her work has influenced the society, and the world. We're honored to have you join us."

She nodded. "I know." The debut was short, blunt and totally in character.

Her work has probably doomed humanity... and I'm the only one who can possibly slow it down. She has to be on the hit list.

Dr. Chavez's remark triggered a wry smile from Ansen. "Moving on, I'm sure you all saw the carnage from the mass shooting event in New York."

Liza fought to keep her jaw from clinching. *Callan was supposed to take care of that troublemaker.*

Ansen continued. "While this was a national tragedy, it also hit close to home. My son, Adam, is a regular patron of Chalky's and but for the tragedy of Gwen Blaze's death, he may have been among those killed."

If only...

"Having said that, I'm going to share a detail that makes this society business, demanding a response." Looking straight into the camera, Ansen went public. "Children are at the core of what we stand for. What has not been made known is that one of the young women gunned down was pregnant." He paused as if for effect. "The father of that unborn child was Adam... making one of the casualties my unborn grandchild."

Gasps could be heard from around the world, then Sameer spoke. "I am so sorry to hear of your family's loss, and you're right, it does require a response. What do you propose?"

Oh shit.

He sighed. "Surnames from the past haunt us again. Becky Brown and Kelley Slaughter are close associates of the young man who pulled the trigger. It's time we had a talk with them."

Damn it! Ben Brown's legacy of getting people killed lives on in his spawn of a daughter.

Chavez spoke for the first time. "What is the plan?"

Yes. How bad is this?

Ansen leaned forward. "The two women have gone underground, but we've just located their hideout. As we speak, a team is being assembled to apprehend them. We'll wait for the cover of darkness to detain them… then one way or another, we get answers."

Oh God! I've got to contact Callan… now!

Chavez nodded. "Excellent."

"Thank you for your support." Ansen slowly rubbed his hands together. "I'll have an update soon."

Liza's mind raced, glancing at the clock in the corner of the screen every few seconds, trying to will this video travesty to end. The rest of the virtual meeting was mercifully short and, like the previous time, she made a quick exit to her waiting car. Wasting no time, she was tapping a text to Callan as soon as her rear hit the seat. *Get a team together ASAP. Instruction to follow. Life or death!*

As soon as Liza left, Ansen phoned Dr. Chavez. "Do you think we smoked her out?"

Laughing, Chavez replied. "I could see the blood draining from her face from here."

CHAPTER FIFTY-SEVEN

The call from Silverstone Confidential came a few minutes after noon. Adam's words were cold and hard. "What have you found?"

Clint Broyles' matter of fact delivery reminded Adam of the man's military background. "The two women did a good job going off the grid, that is until Becky Brown turned on her phone this morning. We have a location."

He couldn't contain his smile. "I need to have a conversation with them…soon."

"I thought you might feel that way, so I had a spy drone overfly the cabin they're in. The bad news is that there are eight body heat signatures inside. They've got company."

Adam paced. "I don't want to miss this opportunity. What are our options?"

"Their location is in a wooded area, so we can establish a perimeter without being seen. If their visitors were to leave, then we would be ready to move, with haste. They could be detained by nightfall."

His free hand formed a fist. "I like the sound of that… and I want to be there if it happens. I need to see the look in their eyes."

"We're here for our clients. I'll send GPS coordinates so you can meet us around two o'clock."

"See you then." With the call ended, he pondered whether to

call Ensley. *She'll kill me if I do this...and she'll kill me if she finds out I did this without her. I'm a dead man either way.*

He stared at the phone in his hand and mumbled. "With my luck lately, she *will* find out." He tapped her name on the screen and she answered on the third ring. "I found them."

"No, Adam, don't do this. Let the society handle it."

"Sorry, Ens. It's going down today, and you can't talk me out of it."

There was a long pause. "Then I'm going too. We do this together."

CHAPTER FIFTY-EIGHT

Liza found herself in camo clothing leaning against a tree in a New York wood, two hours outside the city. "I don't see why I need to be here."

Callan had rounded up three men on short notice. "This isn't exactly a well-planned mission, and like I said, if you want it done in such a reckless way, you have to take the same risk as us."

While she understood that logic from his point of view, it was precisely the haphazard planning that made her want to be anywhere but here. "What do we know?"

He pointed a parabolic microphone at the small structure. "We've picked up several voices, so they've got company."

Lifting the binoculars that Callan handed her, she tried to divine who could possibly be with those two, with zero success. "Damn it." She lowered the glasses. "I know for a fact that another team is heading here soon, and if that were them, they would already be gone. If they get those two first, I'm a dead woman. Give me options."

Sweat beaded on Callan's brow. "Liza, this isn't how I do things, and that's the reason I've survived for so long."

Liza glanced at her phone. "Two-thirty. It's decision time." She bit her lower lip. "What if I double the payment?"

Callan pulled out a green and brown splotched army hanky and wiped his forehead. "Are you sure you want to do this? I've got a bad feeling."

Her breathing felt constricted. "I don't *want* to, but I don't have a choice."

Sighing, he laid out the improvised plan. "We have the element of surprise, and we're a small team. I can get us close before they even know what's happening. If the goal is to simply kill everyone inside, we can fill the place full of lead and have a chance."

∞

Adam looked over Clint's shoulder at the video coming in from the nearly silent drone. "That thing is incredible."

Clint nodded. "Yeah. The technology has advanced fast. They…" He stopped talking, then pointed to movement on the screen. "We have company."

Ensley had totally surprised Adam by choosing to join him. "So, let me get this straight. We don't know who's inside with those women, and now there are more people here? Any idea who they are?"

"I don't know who they are, but it's not good. Look."

Adam and Ens squinted at the screen until Adam realized what they were seeing. "I'll say. That's some serious firepower they're carrying." He felt a tingling sensation moving up his spine, ramping his nervous energy even more. "This just got a lot more dangerous."

Ens pushed her hair behind her ear. "Now I'm really glad Maddy is still on the west coast with her father. This is the last place she needs to be."

Clint nodded, then made a recommendation. "It looks like we haven't been spotted, so let's stay hidden and let this play out before making a move."

Ens seconded. "Yeah. No need tipping our hand."

Ansen waited a half-mile away with a second team, ready to swoop in if Liza made a play to kill Becky and Kelley. He spoke into the walkie talkie to the team inside. "Is the Kevlar material in place?"

Kyle Darden, leader of the heavily armored primary team, replied. "Yes sir. It should provide enough protection."

"Good. Spot anything unusual?"

"No sir... wait." Kyle's voice sounded urgent. "Sir, we have a sighting about twenty yards out. What are your directions?"

Ansen glanced at Becky and Kelley sitting in the back seat of the SUV. "See. She intended to kill you." He then spoke to Kyle. "Let them get a few yards closer, then open fire. We're on our way."

∞

The sudden and sustained bursts of gunfire from the cabin caused Adam to startle. He reached for Ensley's hand. "I'm glad we stayed on the sidelines."

Her open mouth told him more than the words that followed. "What the hell?"

Both the team in the field and whoever was in the shack were now firing at each other in non-stop waves. Clint added more information as he pointed to the drone feed. "And now we've got even more company."

Adam and Ensley looked intently at the screen as a large black SUV entered the frame. A sense of familiarity crept in as Adam processed the rapidly changing scene. "Zoom in on the vehicle!"

Clint did as requested, and the image of more armed operators piling out filled the monitor. "I've never seen anything like this. What's going on here?"

"That's my father!" Adam pointed excitedly at the image. "Shit. What's he doing here?"

Clint turned to face Adam. "Tell me this isn't a mafia thing. We don't play that game."

Shaking his head, Adam answered honestly. "It's not the mob. I promise."

"What then?"

Adam realized this was the society taking care of business, like his father told him they would... and he also knew he couldn't tell Clint. "Look, I'm going over there to join him. This is a family thing gone very wrong, and the last place you need to be is here."

Clint blinked hard. "There's a shootout happening over there, and we've been hired to protect you. No way I'm leaving."

Standing tall, Adam tried to sound as mature as he could. "You've been paid in full." Now Adam pointed in the other direction. "And I'm telling you to get the hell out of here for your own good. Understand?"

Clint stared at him with eyes seeming confused by the demand. "You're fucking crazy." With that, he turned and began directing his men. "Retrieve the drone and load up. We're out of here."

Ensley reached for Adam's hand. "I'm going out there with you."

He looked down at her, ready to try and talk her out of that, but saw her dark eyes narrowed, and her jaw set. His shoulders dropped. "I know I can't change your mind, but I wish you would stay here."

"I know." That was all she said until Clint and his crew were gone. "We do this together."

∞

Liza now lay prone in the leaf litter of the forest as bullets whizzed inches above her head. Her right leg ached as blood from a bullet wound seeped onto the ground. Moments ago, those bullets were only coming from the cabin, already killing one of Callan's men. Now they found themselves being attacked from behind as well. Suddenly, everything made sense. *I've been set up.*

Callan yelled above the constant barrage. "We've got to get out of here. It's our only chance. Let's go!"

She lowered her head, knowing that with her injury she wouldn't have a snowball's chance in hell of standing, much less running. Facing reality, she shouted. "I'm a dead woman no matter what. I'll try and hold them off while you and your men make a run for it."

He didn't wait to be told twice as he and the two surviving men made a break for it, running away, deeper into the woods.

Considering her options amid the chaos, she spotted two figures running across the open area only yards away, hardly believing her eyes. *It's two of those monster children. It may be my last day on earth, but at least it will be theirs too.* Taking two calming breaths, she lined up the first shot on Adam. As she did, she heard a voice yelling. "Get down!" then caught sight of another figure out of the corner of her eye, running toward the freaks. *Ansen! Killing the patriarch would be even better!*

Her decision to change targets cost her time, and with amazing speed, Adam had closed the gap between himself and his father. Now lining up her shot on Ansen she squeezed the trigger. *Boom.* The chamber reloaded automatically as she realized her delay had allowed Adam to fully close the distance. Her bullet struck him instead of Ansen, and both Clayborn men fell. In a fraction of a second, she considered the possibility of a through shot that killed them both. *Amazing!*

Hearing Ensley scream, the fantastic possibility of a triple kill thrilled her. *One more shot and whatever happens to me will all be worth it. Boom.* Ensley dropped like a lead balloon.

Those were kill shots. Her mind went to her dead friend, Ben Brown. *That was for you, big guy.*

She hugged the ground, but a moment later it felt as if someone hit her left shoulder with a sledgehammer. Rolling on her back, she reached with her right hand and felt warm, flowing blood. *This is it.*

Rather than slowly bleed out, she analyzed her situation and reconsidered. *I've talked my way out of some tight spots, maybe I can again.* She raised her stained red right hand and shouted. "I surrender!"

The gunfire ebbed, then stopped. She gave herself a silent pep talk as she waited. *No matter what happens today, in the end I stood for what I believed and was willing to die for it. That counts for something.*

CHAPTER FIFTY-NINE

Falling hard as his son crashed into him, Ansen tried to assess the situation as he heard the call of surrender from a woman, and recognized the voice. "That bitch."

As the gunfire fell silent, he rolled his son off of him, then saw his worst nightmare. "No!" Blood was rhythmically oozing from a serious chest wound. He applied pressure and reassured Adam in a shaky voice, fearing the worse. "It's going to be okay, just hang on!"

His son's choked single laugh surprised him. "*I* know that." Adam winced in obvious pain. "And you should too. Now go check on Ens."

Ansen ripped off his shirt and pressed the wad of fabric over the gaping hole. "You're my son. I'm taking care of you first."

Adam pushed his father's hand away. "I'm telling you, I'm going to be alright. Go check on Ens, please!"

Looking in his son's eyes, he saw no fear, only concern for Ensley, so he relented. "Okay, but hold the shirt in place to try and stop the bleeding." Now he scurried a few feet finding Ensley, and she was gasping in pain as well. "Hang in there."

She cursed. "Son of a bitch. This hurts!"

Watching in disbelief, he saw the blood flow begin to slow as her wound started closing. "How?"

She spoke as she removed her hand from the formerly large hole growing smaller by the minute, gritting through clear discomfort. "That's definitely going to leave a mark." She snorted. "No, it's probably not."

Having seen Adam's head wound heal rapidly, he realized he shouldn't have been surprised, but he was. These were wounds that would kill any other human, and they were joking about it. He mouthed words from his heart. "Thank you, Dr. Chavez. I take back every bad thing I've ever said about you."

Kyle Darden shouted. "We have her, Mr. Clayborn."

As hard as their nearly instant healing was to believe, he couldn't deny what was happening right in front of him. With parental fear subsiding, his anger at Liza returned. Ansen waved Kyle over. "Bring her here. We need to have one last talk." He then turned back to the SUV and shouted to the soldier standing guard. "Bring those two as well. They need to be part of this conversation."

Both escorted groups arrived at the same time. Adam had crawled over to Ensley, both now sitting cross-legged, alternating between groans and light laughs. Liza was being held up by two armed men clad in black, looking pale, like she had just seen the ghost of Ben Brown himself. She steadied herself on her uninjured leg as she stared at Adam and Ensley. "That's impossible. Those were two clean shots."

Ansen sent the guards away. "I'll take it from here."

As the soldier walked away, Adam pulled his shirt up, revealing the already partially closed wound. "That was a damned good shot, Mrs. Howard. I'll give you that."

Kelley looked like she was about to faint. "What's happening?"

Reaching for his father's hand, Adam pulled himself up. "You now know the biggest secret in the world."

Liza wobbled, then crumpled to the ground on her knees, her voice weak. "Ben was right, you're monsters. Humanity is doomed."

Ignoring Liza, Ensley took Adam's hand, then pointed at Becky and Kelley as she stood. "What are those two thugs doing here?"

Now it was Ansen who laughed. "Turns out, they're having a special child as well."

Holding her injured shoulder, Liza again spoke in disbelief. "How could you? Your fathers..."

Kelley began to cry. "We didn't know. We were tricked by that evil Dr. Chavez."

Ansen sighed as he drew a pistol from his shoulder holster, turning toward Liza. "You've been trying to kill my son since before he was born, and yet, you were given a second chance. Today, you've forfeited that gift."

The once proud woman stared at the ground in defeat. "I... have...completely...failed."

Nodding, Ansen agreed. "Yes, you have. Kristoff was right to spare you to help heal the society's split, so I don't understand. Why did you take up the reformer beliefs again?"

"Does it matter?" She looked up at Ansen. "Survivor's guilt of being spared while Ben and Ezra weren't...Anger over losing the patriarch selection to you, the first GM father no less...True belief that every modified child born moves humanity one step closer to our demise? Take your pick."

Ansen spoke to the young people. "You may want to step away."

Kelley and Becky took Ansen up on the offer, walking back toward the SUV, while Adam and Ensley stayed put. Adam explained. "She's been linked to almost everything bad that's happened lately, plus she just tried to kill me again. I don't *want* to see this, but I know I *need* to be a witness."

"Goodbye, Liza." Wasting no more time, Ansen fired a single shot into her bowed head.

CHAPTER SIXTY

The ratings always spiked when Larry Knewell had the first three so called 'Designer Babies' on his show. Tonight would be no exception as new anti-GM legislation had failed to pass the senate by a single dissenting vote from Senator Alfonse. He expected a jubilant trio on set to triumphantly trumpet the win. "Congratulations on the political success today. How does it feel to see legislation that would have set limits on college admission for gene-edited students go down to defeat?"

Ensley answered in a voice that was anything but boastful. "Larry, it was a hard-fought battle that we feel fortunate to have won. But we know this was just a skirmish, not the end of the war on our rights. I can almost guarantee that a similar bill will be filed next term."

The host pushed. "Still, a win is a win. Right? Seems as if you have momentum on your side with the top two leaders of WAGE stepping down this week."

A head tilt and sigh preceded Ensley's reply. "Becky Brown and Kelley Slaughter said they want to spend more time with their child, and I understand that. It doesn't mean the organization they left is going to change. In fact, the newly announced leader seems even more determined to treat us as second-class citizens. That's not something to celebrate."

Hoping to inject more energy into the interview, Larry turned to Madeline Blaze. "Maddy, I understand you're back in the studio recording new music. When is your next tour? I'm sure your fans will again fill stadiums."

There was more than a touch of melancholy in her response.

"I'm hitting the road next month, dedicating the shows to my mother. In addition to new material celebrating her life, I'll also be performing some of her classics. She was a great artist, mother and wife. I miss her so much."

Larry's head lowered. "I miss her, too. We didn't always see things eye to eye, but who could resist her energy? Please accept my deepest condolences for your loss." His head raised. "How's your father holding up?"

The first hints of positivity edged into the show. "He's thrown himself into his quest to find a cure for Huntington's Disease. Working with Dr. Chavez, he feels a lot closer, and that's terrific news."

"Wonderful! Please give him my regards and well wishes in such a challenging time." She nodded as Larry turned to the final member of the trio. "Adam, I understand big things are happening with your business. What can you share of your success?"

Adam's demeanor was his usual television calm. "That's right, Larry. My microbank has just surpassed ten million clients... and remember, most of these patrons had previously been locked out of the financial system."

He felt the show finally gaining momentum and wanted to end the segment on a high note. "I also hear that there's romance in your life now."

Both Adam and Ensley blushed as he reached for her hand. "That's right." They looked into each other's eyes as the camera pushed in. We're officially dating and I've never been happier."

Having the show arc finish where he wanted, Larry wrapped the segment in his typical style. "Each of our lives have moments of blissful highs and crushing lows. That's the human condition. As you've seen tonight, that's true even if your genes have been modified to provide almost every advantage in life. At some point each of us face discrimination, loss, success and love."

Turning to camera two, Larry continued. "Having said that, these three people are different...special. They opened the door through which millions of others have followed, producing genetically perfect humans." He leaned toward the camera, and his voice lowered. "Now a new phenomenon has begun. With today's announcement of animal DNA being introduced into humans we've crossed into completely new territory, and no one is confident in predicting where this development will lead. Stay tuned as we next hear from the scientists who have achieved this feat, as well as from some activists who continue the fight against all genetic modification of humans. It promises to be another exciting episode of *Rare Air*.

Bree and Ansen had watched the show with a mix of pride and apprehension, mostly agreeing with Larry. Bree summed up her feelings. "They've all turned out to be exceptional young people, but I know the coming years are only going to get more challenging. I guess all parents worry about their children's welfare and happiness."

Ansen agreed. "I'm glad we have the society to help level the playing field. It's clear that the challenges faced so far pale in comparison to what's to come. Are you sure you won't take one of the empty council seats? I could use your support."

A chill ran down her spine. "I'll always support you, but you know how I hate the politics. Instead, I'll just continue to make the world a better place."

Putting his arm around her, he leaned in for a quick kiss. "We do already make a good team, and congratulations on those new numbers on average global temperatures. You're making real progress."

Her pride was evident. "We've played our part, that's for sure." Her thoughts returned to the society. "Since I'm a hard 'no' on joining the council, who are you considering?"

He was quiet for a moment. "Don't hate me, but I've been thinking about Adam."

"What! He's too young, too inexperienced! Besides, it's proven to be a dangerous position lately and he's our only child."

The two nods were quick. "You're absolutely right, but there are other things to consider."

"This better be good, or I may have to use the wife veto."

Ansen laughed at her made-up procedural tool. "Wife veto? Huh, I'll have to look that one up."

"I'm being serious. Why would you consider Adam for that seat?"

"Think about it, Bree. Every day more GM society children are born. They are our future, and we need to hear their voice as we move into that future."

"Okay, that makes sense... sort of. But that's not enough of a reason for me."

Ansen moved to face her. "You weren't there, in the woods with Liza."

"I've heard the story." Her voice now small.

"But you didn't see it. Adam saved my life, and both he and Ensley were shot through with silver-dollar-sized holes. I was amazed as they healed even faster than when Adam's head was fractured. And they laughed as their wounds began closing in front of our eyes. I still barely believe it, and I was there. So, if being on the council is dangerous, who could be better prepared for the risks? Look, GM members will make up the majority of the society in thirty years or less, so we need to bring one of them onto the council soon."

She knew what her husband was saying was true, but after everything they had been through, she was still afraid of losing the child she loved so dearly. "Do you think they have other powers we have yet to see? Other ways to protect themselves?"

A wry smile graced his face. "If so, I'm sure Dr. Chavez will only tell us when she's ready."

The End

Thank you for reading *Designer Babies Volume Two, Growing Pains.* If you liked the book and would like to continue reading the series, *Volume Three, Passing the Torch,* is available now. Also, I would be grateful if you would consider putting up some stars on the Amazon store page. Even better, if you have time, I'd appreciate a review. They are the life blood of independent authors, and your review would have a huge impact on my book's visibility to other readers.

David Witt